KICKS

Jeremy Reed

KICKS
Jeremy Reed
ISBN 1 871592 15 1
Copyright © Jeremy Reed 1993
All rights reserved
First published 1994 by
CREATION BOOKS
83, Clerkenwell Road
London EC1
Tel/Fax: 071-430-9878

ACKNOWLEDGEMENTS:

*The Paris Review, Lovely Jobly, The Rialto, Poetry Wales, Best Of
Bowie Now, Temenos, Sphinx, Tabla, The Poetry Project, Slow
Dancer, Lust, Resurgence, The Shelf Life Of Bernard Stone,
Blood And Roses, Klaonica.*

Some of these poems first appeared in the following booklets:
Around The Day Alice, Orange Pie: Carnivorous Arpeggio
Press. *Volcano Smoke At Diamond Beach*: Cloud. *Anastasia*:
Ink Sculptures.
Blue Sonata was privately published by Alan Ladd.

Photography: John Robinson
Make up: Anita

KICKS

For Pascale

A diva a day
Keeps the boredom away

— *Marc Almond*

When I was young, I could not have accepted as a lyrical poet anyone weighing more than ninety-nine pounds.

— *Theophile Gautier*

There is no other origin of beauty than the wound, singular, different for each person, hidden or visible, which every man keeps inside him, which he preserves and where he withdraws when he wants to leave the world for a profound but passing solitude.

— *Jean Genet*

CONTENTS

BLUE PRELUDE

The Blues

Even the light's de-toned. I'd wish less tilt
in how I see. I'm like an ear of maize
at half slant, twigging from the stalk.
Slice a tomato on a patterned plate

and there's a clash. The reds won't settle down.
They want an undivided white or blue.
I feel that edgy, like a storm won't break
but flickers with long yellow antennae.

I smell the words when they arrive,
they brush me with the crackle of a wasp.
The radio's unconsolatory,
a cracked voice sings, 'What a wonderful world'.

Often the distance between me and things
seems disproportionate. I cannot reach
across that space. Reality
is like the memory of a beach

that burnt so whitely just three months ago,
and when evoked is mostly in shadow,
the people undistinguished by detail,
blotches like snow settling on snow.

It is a sort of blues, but more oblique
than down mood slumps, pockets that last a day.
I'll kill it by exposing its habits,
slicing a tomato as casual play.

Taxi To The End Of The World

And it was nothing, so the driver said,
digesting elephant steaks or zebra,
his stomach open like a corolla,
discussing protein, toxins, Manhattan,
extreme eating because the planet's dead,

and he'd be going back after this ride
to the old cities, his box apartment.
'Someone's got to stay': my presentiment
was of him looting, fisting out diamonds
from display cards. Our wheels skirted the tide

and there were cattle and a family
knee-deep in water looking for a place
to cross; a bridge sunk beneath the surface
of rising waters. We went into hills,
making a detour to meet with the sea

on the last coast. The man spoke of nomads,
straggling tribes who had marched on the desert
listening for instructions, ways to alert
themselves to power, and of politicians
making suicide-pacts on pyramids.

We passed the first shacks put up on this coast.
Numeral calculations done in blood
were wildly calligraphized on white wood.
A lion-tamer instructed his child,
a group of long-haired men sat around lost;

and here the taxi stopped, he wouldn't go
right to the end, and he was obstinate.
He spoke of dangers and he had a date
that evening; love and barbecued camel,
one of the last from a blackmarket zoo.

Zamora Institute

He inserts a mauve contact lens and checks
his reconstructed features; collagen
implants, liposuction; he's angular
and out-profiles Michael Jackson.
Outside, a metal tree shaped like a star

scintillates in the dangerous UV light.
A child sits in a sculpted conifer
and walkie-talkies his robotic toy.
The real park lions are lobotomized.
The big one sleeps curled up on a parked car.

And daily, new arrivals come to stay
and attend lectures. They will recreate
themselves; dismantle knowledge of their past,
adopt names given by their instructors
and stand outside a compression-sealed gate

awaiting admission into a cult
for the re-formed. No-one may ever speak
of the initiation. Some remain
inside for years and return as children
who walk off fearless across a dust plain

towards the lost cities; the fabled worlds
where earlier ancestors lived and died.
He checks his memory loss on a screen,
the red digits read cancelled and the green
matter to be revised. The optimum

is 0.5 green. And still the children play
their adult games before lectures, and ten
analysands strike out beneath the trees,
headed for pre-initiation jabs
they walk clean through the sleeping lion's den.

Billie Holiday

Reworking cadence, when she finds the note
it's always different, singing without words
at the Apollo, letting her drift float

with the blue smoke plumes from a cigarette.
Style's in her spacing of words, Lady Day
a white flower in her hair, leading the set

wherever breath dictates, a mussed lipstick
tinting the song, one hand placing a glass
back on the piano top. It's not a trick

to catch the spotlight, but a need. Up there
her isolation is complete, she finds
a means to centre it, and takes us where

there's consolation for a spike-heeled fall
into back alley junk. *Gloomy Sunday*
is slowed to speech. Leaning against the wall

her back contains the storm. She feels the past
as a pivotal hurricane, and lets
the saxophonist punctuate the cast

of figures she inhabits; it is hard,
maintaining poise, creating out of pain,
bowing out at the end as a reward.

Edith Piaf

The stage is my one shelter from the world,
invulnerability around the wound
of red roses thrown at my feet
at the Olympia or Bobino.
The spotlight integrates dualities,
I am a girl again out on the street,

singing to stay alive, singing to eat,
my cracked saucer extended to the crowd.
Out here, I'm safe; my drugged, tormented past
stays in abeyance for an hour.
The music insulates. That is my way

of sobering the manic chimeras;
the morphine I'll needle into a vein,
the scenes I'll create later, wedging jewels
and money I've earnt down a Paris drain,

the hangers-on who I can't turn away,
crowding the dressing-room. Sometimes I scream
and realize that this isn't a dream,
it is my life, this broken champagne glass

got like that when I tore my dress
and set fire to my hair. My voice goes out
to reverse fortunes, losers and winners
in love and life; the poor, the deeply hurt
are closest to my heart. I'll leave this earth

with nothing, I who was born in the street,
swaying on stage to keep upright,
praying I'll get through and it's the last night.

Around The Day, Alice

An aircraft's filming ad props in a field,
fibre glass bottles blown to a man's height
are there awaiting a new-age Alice
in thigh boots and a micro-skirt
to decamp from a car, point a mirror
in which white rabbits snow across the glass.
Her driver is a purple hare.

I skirt around the edges of a pond,
the submerged car is flickered through
by trout fry – a leisurely pony-tail
formation, then bright zinging dots
scattering morse into shadow.
A fisherman sits on the lake
dreaming he could do this without a boat.
Just meditate on a dark blue cushion
and count individual clouds.

I listen to my radio
and jump the years, forward and back,
guitars travel down the air-waves.
I lie face up. Alice will be here soon,
picking the big white daisies in the grass,
setting a red check tablecloth,
a purple hare stand looking through the glass.

Far Out

The rumours of his being everywhere,
but never seen, or nowhere, black on black,
proliferate, multiply to a film
in which enigmatic footage repeats
his visual changes, or the camera slows

to meditation on a door
infused with white light, or a lifting jet
aimed from Kennedy to a red sunset,
a blank frame punctuating every three
as a phased, abstract possibility,

putative whereabouts. The gold limo
was found parked by the surf, all doors open,
a transvestite chauffeur dead at the wheel,
a lexicon of scarlet roses spread
across the sand formed 'Nowhere left to go

is somewhere in the universe'. Ashes
had been packed into a shoe-box
and placed on the rear seat, and there were marks
of a helicopter ridged on the sand.
The ocean was thirty shades of mid-blue.

And later there were sightings, someone seen
behind dark glasses in Zürich, or high
on anonymity threading the streets,
the air diamond November, hunched into
a collar-up black greatcoat with a green

tie escaped, just a right touch of panache.
The mystery stays and is part of the age,
the myth of the undying, a gold car
left by the wave-line, and a fiction born
around the many faces of a star.

Transparency

A pink horse moves into the blue painting,
making acquaintance with new mental space.
Just turn me back to front, she says,
my panties are sheer black, sheer white;

you make of me two people anyway.
She walks around the room like that,
posturing a translucency.
A white cloud sits on a mauve summit like a hat.

And there's no urgency to claim
the fulness she offers. Slipped out of jeans
she likes to tempt. Her triangle is shaved.
The harmonics of space are curved not flat.

The painted horse indicates possibilities
of knowing that its counterpart
won't achieve through reality.
The things I learn are what I'd like to see.

More light shows through her stretched transparency.
The brush vibrates on impasto.
She bends over an armchair casually
finding her fingers where they want to go

in search of endings which are an object,
a record sleeve, a magazine.
The horse can't see behind its head
development locate a dab of green.

Florist

She tells me things about train timetables
I never know, not just the Russian ones,
but branchlines, ways to reach a certain place
between a town, a bamboo field in flower,

and a yellow cottage called Question Mark.
Her red carnations frostily propose
I look towards the white pleated with pink.
We never think the undersides throw dark

shadows on something, like we lack the map
to use the far side of the moon
as a meditation point. What's beneath
the feet, and what's observable out there?

The pointed tulips occupy a gap
in conversation, hinting as they do
at purple, yellow tongues they'll keep upright
until their last eventful surrender

as fragments on a table. Her red mouth
is so overtly sensuous I aim
erotic imaginings at her lips.
Birds and a train are somewhere heading south.

I think later of complex directions
she keeps inside her head, her ringed left hand
smoothing a leather skirt, and all the flowers
a moment upside-down in a headstand.

Saturdays

The letter comes from Montreal
coincidental with my snipping one
red peony, triple fist-sized, soft knuckles
tumbling compactly from a crown
to pinker, lighter edges at the fringe,
the limit that petals can go
before the snap, the giving out.

Sunlight bounces through the room like a ball,
a solar event striping the carpet.
I make myself notes, NB don't forget
to be the right person today
and not the other. It is Saturday,

more space, expansive light, and later tea
with Loredana, whose fifties glasses
might be a period piece from St Tropez,
the actress wearing white high heels
down to the beach. Rugs, orange towels arranged.

I read the letter. There are red tulips
invade the text, tulips perhaps clearer
for the Canadian air, and I pursue
your narrative, encounter a mountain
you see from your yard, how it goes on up
taking the eyes with it, two blue insects
examining the imaginary view.

Foreign Affairs

The bags are tagged for travel. Somewhere, now,
the ambassador parks his car outside
a whitewashed bungalow along the coast.
The woman's inside, zipping up her skirt,
smoothing the creases, lifting up her hair,

letting it fall. A foreign town attracts
for what we think we'll find, but never do,
characteristics of a place
we recognize as the one spot on earth
where we can live and perhaps never die.
The ambassador lies back on the bed,
the woman unzips her skirt from behind,
slowly, affording him the view
she knows excites.

                    We've never been to where
we're flying on this summer's day,
the clouds are roofing over the airport,
but it's always the other side
of life for which we're aimed, and now she kicks
one shoe off, then the other, turns around,
and he is waiting with his many tricks.

Seven Admissions

1

The trees are equal to the wind tonight.
Our thoughts are in a foreign town. One dream
gives the lemon wings – and the orange flight.

2

What if the owl contrived to get inside
our room. A white owl with emerald eyes.
Would there be head-space in which we could hide?

3

When we last spoke, we suggested the sea.
Your white triangle underneath a white
thong-backed V'd isosceles bikini.

4

Why did the swan have oars crossing the lake,
white oars for a black swan? The image stayed
on my dream view-finder like a snowflake.

5

Writing means making a trek to China,
crossing so many mental continents,
wearing a mountain as a tiara.

6

Adjusting my thoughts, you are luminous,
throwing a planetary light on the room.
Your tongue flickers and it's adventurous.

7

You kiss me through a square of silk. A grape
breaks open in my mouth. I know you now,
sinuous, pliant in your feline shape.

Dressing Marilyn Monroe

The line should never disagree
or adopt its own tangent. It's her curves
create the dress, give shape to gold lamé,
the flesh-coloured buttons sewn into her net bra
accentuate the nipples, it's a trick
adopted from Marlene Dietrich,
conical breasts prominently engaged
in a deep V'd halter neck, or she's stitched
into the tightness of her skirt,
not even a suspender strap
smudging the contour, despite two black seams
vertical from calf to ankle;
and it's the aesthetic of creating a nude
fully dressed on high heels allows us to
imagine we know her body
out of a swimsuit, her left breast escaped
from a snapped shoulder-strap or in fishnets

leading us up a tall staircase.
Mostly she's an illusion. We impose
the image we expect, the full length dress,
one knee angled forward, hands on the hips,
or think of her making up, dark lipstick,
tinctures of Chanel Nº 5,
hair in a towel, nothing but silk panties
on her tanned body and the swimming pool
outside the window shaped like a pink rose.

For Blond Hair

I sat in a treetop. The world was right
and very far. Was it an April day
I saw you bent to one knee retrieving
a bracelet snapped on a link-chain, your mind
so fully concentrated on your hand,
you occupied that space, fitted your thought
without intrusive overlap, your hair
losing its parting as it fell
creating shadow. I remember that,
hair the colour of childhood sand.

That time, I used to study from a height,
now I send poems up into the sky
and have them stay there against gravity.
I like to place my subject in the air,
lift a forest into the clouds,
balance my chair and table on the wind.
Today, I protract my itinerary,
linger in bookshops, a harbour alley,
grow excited over fashion displays,
an orange jacket, a black tulip skirt,
and know I'm searching, looking out again
for you, or someone like you, sunlit-blond,
shocking my senses back to the story
in which the grass was blue and the sky green
and your image was brighter than the sun
finding a leopard sleeping in a tree.

Threads

They never link coherently,
not even late night, when the one story
we try to unify seems to converge
on a common landmark, a headlit tree
that once surprised us in the dark

for being splashed with paint, we on the road
searching for our country hotel,
that place where somebody dreamt of a horse
so packed with bees it buzzed, and in their dream
they led it to a crossroads where it spoke,
the bees escaping individually,
the creature decomposing. Bones and ash.

And wasn't there that other time
we found a filing cabinet in a field,
battered, glaucous, the colour of amphibians,
the thing was marooned in a ditch,
its contents rifled? In the clear blue light
we felt compelled to carry it away.
Sometimes I go upstairs to the attic
and check if it's still there. The curved black seams

behind your legs are another journey
I'll follow when our narrative stops short,
and now I hear you in another room,
call out, 'Pick up the thread, and come find me.'

Micro-Climate

We sit, backs to the world, facing the sea,
conscious the ultraviolet burns. I read
Kundera's block-shaped *Immortality*,

its snap shots of the deconstructed great
making death seem more human. When we die
we're recomputerized and have to wait

our serial if we return. Right now
the author's drinking coffee in his flat
wondering if it happens anyhow,

for we're all fictions, faces on a screen.
I'd like to find a drug to turn that round.
Acid will only make a red sky green.

We travel light. Thistles grow by the sand,
blue testicles voodooed by greenish pins.
This might be the place for Goethe to land

out of Kundera's novel. Now he'd hear
the Cure's *Disintegration* menacing
the air waves from the other couple near

this gritty hollow tucked under the cliff.
The surf's receding; black, carbonized stumps
of a drowned forest show. Another riff

is underlined with bass. This is our day
with its connectives, wirings into death.
We wouldn't have it any other way.

Pink Lemonade

The ex-pilot half propped up in the bar,
still speaks of his imbalance – altitude –
he can't come down; the silver in his head
just fuzzes. Stuttgart, Rome, New Mexico,
disquiet at the Bermuda Triangle,

sometimes, cocaine which stood him on his head
in mid-flight, 30,000 feet,
a blow-job coming into Kennedy,
he isolates these cameos. The heat
outside has the street seem a white mirage;
the cars double on themselves. There are two
to each cloned driver. It's better that way.
He drapes his flying jacket and his red
bandana is like a hippie's
obsolete vestige of Woodstock.

His friend is a redundant astronaut
trainee. Someone who never knew blast-off,
but went through the ground motions of orbit.
Today, they're going somewhere in one mind,
a blended, unified, trajectory,
a mind-trip. Something will be realized.
He says their eyes turn square green at the find.

Live and Do

A dust-storm blows out of the red valley,
nothing, but as in Georgia O'Keefe,
cow's horns up high in a bare tree,
the civilized gone on the move to find
expression somewhere else, mutate the gene

so that they never die. They put up towns
and move on hurriedly, a trail of cars
nosing across the desert, continents,
their children are born from televisions
and step out of the screen. The ones who stayed

behind watch dust sanding their every view,
and up above them the three purple stars
which seem to move closer to earth each day
vibrate like pulsars. Someone finds a book,
but reading's changed. The words don't fit the mind,

they dot around like flies. The stadium
constructed for open air festivals
is a ruined arena. The last time
someone plugged in their power, it was Neil Young
burning the air with electricity,

directing a hurricane from the stage.
The storm ionizes latent current,
it swipes ten million pingpong balls around
inside the brain. The two painting a shack
earth themselves by lying flat on the ground.

The migrants dismantle their shanty town,
guard secrets of the chromosome, and stay
monogamous. Their children are sci-fi
mutants. This week their group heads for Tibet,
and big white flowers fall out of the sky.

Fruit Dish

Espace, brûlant compotier.
– *René Char*

Dark bees in the lavender. Noon is indigo,
honey; nectar responsive to fire
from the aromatic bee.

If you look beyond, the horizon's a white frame,
a blank that will deepen to blue.
Imagine a fruit-dish balanced there,
red apples, yellow pears, a lime,
a black necklace of grapes, an allusion

to space as occupied. I cannot hear
the valley for the heat,
the stream for shadow.
Opposite tonalities. I cannot hear my speech
inside your mouth.

Space as a burning fruit-dish,
and the whisper of your red bra
disclosing apples, mauve areolas
the colour of anemones.

White Paper

My writing on it builds a cenotaph.
Language that's deconstructed by the years
lives as a transient autograph,

no permanence. I never knew the trees
on which I wrote. Sometimes I have the dream
I've slept through Canada, eyes wide open
on mental space inside a car.
With words I am a different sort of passenger,
I go along with them, but don't know why
or where they need to travel. There are trees
encountered in that journey. Blue and red
and yellow; they are by the road
and nowhere special. I am on the line;

the marks I leave behind me sting like bees.

Map Making

It's about reinvention, star clusters
expanding into redshift, light signals
travelling away from the universe,
and how the ordinary is transformed,
the street corner curves suddenly into
a town called Hexagram, an eight-sided,
forested place there for discovery,
its people listening to an eighth sense
with the immediacy of radio,
and on the outskirts there's a crystal sea
through which one views proliferating ferns,
riotous fauna, exploding seed pods
turning that instant into flowers. And words
convey the transformation. I can see
three separate skies, a white, a green, a red,
form a triptych, three windows into space,
an expansive cosmogony.
Nothing's fixed, or identifiable
except by how it changes, the wonder
of making maps for alternative worlds,
the real ones in which imagery
stands out like markings on the ocelot,
and the way forward leads out of a line
into a spiral, takes me where snowflakes
are shaped like strawberries and fall red-hot.

Scarlet Begonias And Blue Thoughts

Their red's so excruciatingly brilliant –
the scarlet begonias, meringue-seashells
floppily open like full peonies

and private. Coloured that way by the light,
they take the eye there; but my thoughts are blue
in meeting their solar target.
And other things are happening. She's there
my distracted neighbour, always alone
and sunning on a balcony,
a Euro-Japanese, eyes averted,
a white scarf in her blueblack hair.
She reads. Her eyelashes are butterflies.

I take in spaces of being alive;
I need so much and so little and both
are disproportionate. She goes inside
and draws a bedroom curtain, a green swish
that has her naked, while I hunt for clues
as to why red flowers dramatically
evoke a down-mood evening-blues.

Star-Map

A purple curtain's drawn in the white house
opposite. An invading clump of trees
is often the dark blue-green that Magritte
uses to lodge a crescent moon
in foreshortened perspective.
                                    'We're like that,'
you say, 'we blank out visuals for the surety
of space we turn to secrecy;
and what will happen if we go too far
inside the private fantasies
with which we instruct each other?' A star
is visible above their house,
a mineral starfish twinkling glacially.
It's the coming of a compact blue night.

They've left a red chair on the balcony
where she suns in the afternoon, dress off,
dark glasses, a minimal bikini.
Beyond that house the air is wider still
for no obstruction – it is grass country,
a wind that smells of horses. We let in the dark

and watch their screened off privacy.
Later, we'll revert to parameters
which are our own confinement, and pretend
we can still see their house and beyond that
a star-map open to a conjectural end.

Tennis

The tennis court hedged round by cypress trees
was white dust in the summer night.
'These red elbow length gloves with these red shoes
matching the scarlet of my toes,
are all I'll wear' she says; 'the rest is stet:
people will have to imagine my clothes.'
Her friend sucks at a sugar cube,
angles a hat; she's thinking of the night
they played tennis in driving hail,
so many frenetic pearls buzzing by,
the pink fluorescent ball acquiring height
and staying there, a motionless planet
which was still suspended, waiting to drop
one unexpected rainy day.
She'll play in nothing but a hat,
the sort of creation that preoccupied Horst,
and spotted sneakers. They are ready now;
the dark is underlit by a white light,
and in the drive they make out a parked car.
Doubles? One red glove round one black,
they go to find out who their partners are.

Big Shifts

The coast's magenta. There's a yellow hut
couched on the sands in a reality
translated out of Paul Klee's small harbour,

no swimmers anywhere, the sea
an oyster coloured watered-silk. 'It's ten
o'clock,' he says, 'in any century,
not mine, not yours.' And she looks into space,
expecting clock hands on the sun,
the punctual aircraft to arrive,
bringing them news of how the others live
in Yellow Chasm, Diamond Falls, Sirocco Road.

They pick up starfish, a folded *Le Monde*
used as a prop for a sunbather's head.
The date's been bleached out by the sun.
That was when people read the days
as continuity. They sit and wait:

she eats a yellow pear, watches him swim,
and anyhow the plane is late.

White

1

He's shooting across white Ballardian sands,
the camera open on a mirage scene
in which Marilyn Monroe cracks her zip,
folds her white dress over her arm and leads
a lover into a ruined hotel.
The man is seen from behind; a scorpion
tattooed on his bottom, a snake's
a red river inked on his spine.

2

The air's so silent it's like the inside
of sleep: the dream is all action, no sound
accompanies the raging fire
burning the sleeper's house; a popping shell,
white walls split with an earthquake's flaw.

3

The sands again; they lift up dusty wings
announcing storm. A fighter jet drops down.
That's Marilyn standing in white panties
at the open window. Her lover's gone.
The building decomposes for the lens.

4

White dunes. Three white dinghies turned upside down,
the sea lost somewhere like a blue
that memory can't recreate.
I find the film-director sitting there,
nursing a foot, a bloodstained boot.
I help him up to the summit
and we are facing another country,
white sands behind us, and in front
a white city built in the 23rd century.

Elegy

I see you as you were five years ago,
and leave imagination improvise,
you were too trusting and worldly naïve
to take stock of the plague. How could you know

sexual transmission was synonymous
with AIDS, you who lived reclusively,
aestheticism under wraps, and yet
went out at night to join anonymous

circles of outlaws grouped beneath the trees,
and lacerated at orgasmic pitch
wanted to burn, rush when the popper broke
so coming irritated as though bees

were planting red-hot needles in your skin ...
One side of you; so many memories,
the sea-front cottage you inherited,
and your aunt's jewels, the diamonds, sapphire pin

worn in a floppy blue St. Laurent tie.
I see you lying in a small bedroom
surrounded by packing crates, one window
admitting the sea, the other the sky's

lazy blue happening. You had your place,
and summers losing at Monte Carlo,
always the risk, edging the danger line;
and now I think back to your former face,

the one unravaged by cancer, the things
you held so dear which have grown meaningless,
and hope they've placed beside your bed the cold
tropical fires in your familiar rings.

Remnants

'So many disconnected threads. My life
lacks finish,' so she tells an orange blob
unsettled on the canvas, and a knife

ruches an ultramarine impasto.
The surface texture is a cross-blown sea.
A woodlouse makes tracks on the boards below,

house-searching, got in from the leaf stripped cold.
Her diary is 300 mini-films,
dates, cafes. 'Now that orange flips to gold,'

she paints by self-instruction, 'and a green
oblong settles as a lagoon; the cube's
gone underwater as a ruin seen

by fish, a special red fish passing through.'
Luncheon today means going to the sea,
her dealer dressed in white against a blue

immensity of sky; a rooftop place.
'Yellow, for the fish's raised dorsal fin,'
the man she meets never has the same face,

some days he's older, younger, in between.
'The blue is perfect, the yellow and red
owe everything to that capricious green.'

She stands back in tight jeans. Parentheses
between pictures are when she lives. Inside,
the tension hums like a clenched fist of bees.

Nasturtiums

A bitter, peppery scent,
and perfect for the watercolorist –
an orange sun parasoled by green leaves
that finds the yellow in the flower's eye,

much like a jacket lining seen
as intermittent splashes. Saffron silk.
Watching their leaves I think of cinema,
a Japanese street scene in Kyoto –

so many green umbrellas, and the ariel shoot
resembling undulating lily pads,
a canvas turtle marching down the street.
Nasturtiums in early autumn

glower in their orange swimsuits
redder by tones than pumpkin,
almost the colour used by Klee
as wax on his 'sealed letter'.

They're a bright incentive to learn
how visuals co-ordinate,
give a woman green hair and yellow eyes
and a nasturtium on each breast;

the rest is imagination, but her skirt
is orange satin. They open out like pansies
in a water-glass.
Their thin stems are coloured like green hay-grass.

BOWIE BALLARD WARHOL

Film Takes

1

A black sky above a white earth. The introductory voice effects to Bowie's *Sound And Vision* anticipate a silver Lamborghini being driven in a dust-cloud across the landscape. Several aluminium pyramids show on the horizon. As the camera zooms in so the giant image of Warhol, hands placed over his cock, is cut across by lightning.

2

Bowie is seen leaning up against the base to a pyramid. He lights a cigarette in slow motion, his gelled hair falling in strands across his forehead. He appears to be waiting for something or someone. He watches a shooting star travel across space before breaking into song. He sings *The Speed Of Life* while the camera angles in on Ballard wearing dark glasses behind the wheel of the Lamborghini.

3

The passenger seat is empty, but the camera tracking finds the novelist looking behind him. Monroe is sitting in the rear-seat, her fishnet-stockinged legs arched up high with Bowie sitting next to her in a silver dress as the music changes to *Ashes To Ashes*.

4

When the scene changes, the car is seen burning on an area of wasteland. Warhol is filming the metallic pyre, while Ballard films Warhol and Bowie films Ballard. Arc intrudes into the picture. He carries a mannequin with a grotesquely erect penis and deposits it in the fire. Fighter jets crash over while Bowie breaks into *Heroes*.

5

The interior of a hotel suite. The room is full of masks and mannequins. Ballard is examining a blueprint. Warhol toys with a rotating square globe. Bowie sits in a corner, writing into a word processor. Someone stripped to the waist in tight jeans, stands painting with his back to the company. When he turns round his face is a tin can.

6

Warhol is viewed silkscreening in the desert. He is working on his wrecked car series, while Ballard looks on as a detached spectator. Dressed in a black leather jacket, black shades, a striped tie tucked into jeans, the artist is seen transforming images to a canvas painted with a single gloss of livid colour. *Vertical Orange Car Crash, Green Disaster Twice, Purple Jumping Man, Lavender Disaster* – the poetics of these lavender, pink, mint-green and orange paintings are obsessively magnified in clear, blurred or misaligned images. Ballard stares fixedly at the burning cars repeated twenty times on a single canvas.

7

Warhol is viewed in bed with Mr. X. The man lies face down to the pillow so as to remain unidentified. A Chanel N° 5 bottle is enlarged to the point of being the only object in the room.

8

Music blows across Ballard shopping at a late-night supermarket. It is Stacey Heydon's guitar intro to *Station To Station* which follows the writer from the delicatessen to the wines and spirits positioned before check-out. When he comes out into the High Street the figure of Arc as a pilot with his long hair tied back in a pony-tail follows Ballard across the traffic stalled by a green go-light. The pilot splits into a multiple succession of clones. The sky registers a ruby and turquoise detonative flash as a helicopter nosedives into a concrete television block. It breaks up into a suspended fall-out of burning debris.

9

Bowie clippage as the Ziggy androgyne in his farewell concert at the Hammersmith Odeon in 1973 is interspersed with the delirium of crowds storming the car in which his double is driven away. As the car accelerates through urban streets the face at the wheel is seen to be Ballard's.

10

Shots of Marilyn stripping in the Grand Hotel are replayed in a voyeuristic sequence. Her glass sheer stockings are run off her legs as silk cocoons. She stands facing the mirror in a deep black lace suspended belt and black panties. On her bottom two red lipstick *f*s are made to imitate Man Ray's photograph: *Ingres' Violin.*

11

Arc is seen narrowing his camera between Marilyn's legs. On the black counterpane to their bed are arranged the miniature German officers discovered as a collector's toys in a felt-lined case in a bedside drawer. Each wears a swastika on his uniform. The lens blows them up to life size. A swastika is positioned above Marilyn's shaved pubis. Beside her is a copy of the Bowie bootleg, *Nazi Heroically.*

12

Bowie's *Station To Station* slashes across Lou Reed's *White Light White Heat.* The visual accompaniment is that of a mannequin dressed as a clown in scarlet puffed sleeves and a pointed gold hat. In its left hand stands a model of Adolf Hitler, arm raised in salute.

13

The labyrinthine anfractuosities of the stone forest are explored. Coral steeples, spires resembling Giacommeti sculptures, environmental art, Martian graffiti.

14

Ballard stands looking up into the glide-ways. A Jumbo is beginning its descent over the city. Edited into this are shots of Yves Saint Laurent in his white cotton over-jacket, concentratedly sketching at his board, surrounded by Walter Glod robots.

15

A coffin-shaped map of New York indicates in scarlet lettering the places that Andy Warhol frequented. They flash up with the delayed time spacing of information relays at an airport. Bloomingdale's – Lexington Avenue, Vito Giallo's Antique Shop – 966 Madison Avenue, Jewellery District – West 47th Street, Le Cirque – 58 East 65th Street, Trump Tower – 725 Fifth Avenue, F.A.O. Schwartz toy shop – 767 Fifth Avenue. Warhol is seen handing out copies of *Interview* to New York passers-by. A junkie in a red fur coat stops by, opens it to show that she is wearing nothing but stockings. When her lowered head is raised to camera level the face is seen to be Marilyn's.

16

The fragmentary narrative moves to the ruined villas along the coast. Gap-roofed, missing walls, figurative totems lodged amongst sunflowers in the gardens. The atmospherics build to the sound of Iggy Pop's *Some Weird Sin*, stills of Aleister Crowley seen with Hitler at the Abbey of Thelema, then a series of multiple images depicting the world leaders sitting waiting in a nuclear dug-out for the heat flash. They watch Arc's film, share out the sachets of powdered protein, exchange snapshots and discreetly masturbate. A robot programmed to administer euthanasia shots is screened off in an adjoining cubicle.

17

Another zoom shot of the stone desert. A black sun is mounted on the pointed apex of a reef. A photograph of Jean Cocteau is seen looking out from the centre. He is reading Ballard's *Myths Of The Near Future*. His waist is joined to the celebrated picture of Monroe's white dress blowing up above her thighs.

18

A series of high-speed takes, dubbed over with audio facilities shows Arc's facial planes scrambled into fragmented images; his dark glasses acting as a light reflector. The facets jump into abbreviated visuals. He is blown away into molecular components. When he re-materializes, he is viewed with a solarized body, a turtle shell strapped to his back, his direction a slow crawl towards a disused railway station.

19

Crash. A reconstructed slow replay action of Jayne Mansfield's death. The collisional force of the two cars resembles a log jammed into an alligator's snout. On the billboard by the roadside are posters of James Dean and Albert Camus. A head without a body makes rabbit leaps across the ground and disappears.

20

A green sky over Monte Carlo. Helmut Newton is observed photographing a model on a terrace overlooking the bay. Dressed in black stockings and pivoting on stilettos, she smokes a cigar. The spectator on the opposite roof walks a leopard round the flat rectangle. Its collar and leash sparkle with rhinestones.

21

A girl with her legs arched over her head in a half-somersault runs a red fingernail across her black panties, while the other hand fits inside her stocking top. A mannequin is positioned watching the girl; an erect silver phallus strapped into place. The figure of Warhol standing behind the girl is making his own obsessive film centred on the silver dildo.

22

Trisexual accomplishments. A man is seen making love to a woman on a voluminous hotel bed. She is Indonesian. Her black hair falls straight to her waist. She is up on her haunches. He eases in and out of her and is seen drawing a scarlet loveheart in lipstick on her bottom. On the next bed a man in a platinum Warhol wig is blowing another whose cock is sheathed in a star-patterned condom. On the third bed two women engage in sensuous love. The submissive partner beneath is veiled by a black face-net. Her active partner is seen from behind, her tongue flicking over magenta areolas, her skin-tight leather skirt raised above her bottom. The photographic scene blacks out to images of Bowie, Ballard and Warhol staring from a wall in the dark.

SEGMENTING A BLACK ORANGE

On Marc Almond

So much of what a singer does has to be committed to audial memory, that we live with the voice in our head, an intimate form of possession which is far more pronounced than the process of reading, in which our dialogue with the text is a silent one.

If I say, Marc Almond lives in my head, I mean that. Most of my novels have been written while listening to his music, and the engagement is a subtle one, the singer's input arriving at a tangent to the imaginative dimension I am exploring. Listening to a song while writing is like creating in stereo. There's the internal music of the line I am in the process of formulating, and there's the unrelated accompaniment which somehow gets in on the creative act. I find it a good mix. The music provides a stimulating opposition to what would otherwise be an unreprieved discourse with myself.

I came to take a serious interest in Marc Almond's music at the time of the release of his controversial *Torment And Toreros* LP. The latter was savaged by the sort of insensible critics who common to both the music and literary worlds, disparage whatever threatens their personal limitations. So often critics simply define their own vanishing point, and fail altogether to connect with the space that goes beyond it. Almond's suite of songs, held together by a bruised death-wish, and charged by outrage at the commercial pressures surrounding his career with Soft Cell, were lyrical and visionary, spiky with romantic realism, and entered into one's hearing like a panther carrying a rose in its teeth. An album of fine balances, the scalding invective aimed at the music industry in *Catch A Fallen Star* is offset by songs of deep emotional intensity, the resonantly haunting *In My Room* and the dramatically sensitive medley comprising *Narcissus, Gloomy Sunday* and *Vision*. Almond's art was recognizably one of retrieving lyric at a time when the majority of his contemporaries were communicating through anti-literate semiotics. And there was the voice. Untutored, impassioned, resonant with hurt, and already on the way to becoming the incomparably consummate instrument it is today. Anyone disquieted by Scott Walker's untimely withdrawal into silence was compensated by the realisation that Almond had not only arrived, but would go on to supersede Walker's vocal achievements. By the time of recording *You Have*, Almond's brilliant and insufficiently praised single from 1984, the singer had placed himself at the forefront of British vocalists, developing also an uncategorizable style which blended torch singing and cabaret with the more intelligent fringes of rock.

From Baudelaire onwards, by which I mean the beginnings of the modern sensibility, the committed artist has lived at an angle to society. Poets have a particularly hard time due to the lack of any support system, and the negligible performing facilities made available to them. Almond, while belonging to a far richer profession nonetheless inherits the outsider's role. Uncomfortable with any distinct tradition, unwilling to be assimilated into mainstream music, he remains an occupant of edges, a man who is dangerous by reason of his individuality.

Right from the start of his career, with the hugely successful *Tainted Love*, a song that perfectly fitted his persona at the time, Almond has been concerned with selecting material which accords with his voice, and emotional sensibility. Rock music has been dominated by avarice at the expense of lyric. The ability to write good lyrics is a gift given to few, and yet rather than adopt material, it became financially *de rigueur* for bands to write their own. With Almond it has been otherwise. His own genuine writing abilities have gone hand in hand with an inheritance of song. And whether the writer has been Brel, Brecht, Cole Porter, Peter Hamill, or his recent cover of the Charles Aznavour song *What Makes A Man A Man*, Almond has assimilated a European tradition of written as opposed to scrambled lyrics. If you sing notes you need a purposeful lyric content. Almond's suitability to a-capella renditions of song, as well as to Martin Watkins's sensitive piano accompaniment, means that he lives by the resonance of his words. His breath informs our emotions of the conflicting highs and vicissitudes of love, and as such he is the most subtle interpreter of pain, cruelty, awareness of advancing age, death, in other words the whole emotional spectrum which is otherwise the business of poetry. Almond's voice explores the inner fissures, it breaks into us in the manner of segmenting a black orange, and asks that the song become a source of reintegration. And when he takes violence for a subject it's with tempestuous empathy for unequal relationships, as in *The Animal In You* or *Love Amongst The Ruined* where the unrequited lovers are 'Waiting at the station/For our train to ruination.'

The element of compassion for those who differ, namely the gay people, transvestites and transsexuals who inhabit Almond's own songs, is a neglected dimension of his work. Scott Walker's *Big Louise*, a song which Almond was to cover on his *Untitled* LP, was questionably one of the first lyrics built around gender change. But it's an objective portrait, an attempt to perceive how people react to this anomaly, whereas Almond enters direct into the drag scene, and his memorably intuited conjurations of the suffering in *Her Imagination*, *St Judy*, *Exotica Rose*, and *Champagne*, to mention only a few, evoke a world in which drug casualties and suicides are offered as demythicized reminders of the problems involved in gender change. Almond's lines in *St Judy*, 'And if I die before I wake up/I pray the Lord don't smudge my make up', are an elegiac summation of the problems involved in inventing one's sex. These songs should properly be seen as elegies. In *Her Imagination*, the newly-created person who lives on the fourth floor, was before that 'such a happy boy.' And few singers adopt the female persona as successfully as Almond. Material like *A Woman's Story*, *The Heel*, and *St Judy*, are extraordinary for his embodying the part of a wounded female lover. His emotional unification of male and female, animus and anima, is, particularly in a live context, his identification with inner truth. And if *St Judy* elaborates a fictional life of Judy Garland, or any one of the torch singers who Almond has integrated psychologically, then *Champagne* is more minimalistically stark, and portrays the life of a New York drag artist, degraded into strip at a 'low rent nude revue.' Champagne's drug habit and suicide are recounted non-judgementally, Almond's sympathies implying that the majority invariably force minorities into untenable situations as a way of perpetuating the system.

Very few poets have covered a field that Almond has made distinctly his own, the ethos of transvestism and transsexuality. The richly narrated *L'Esqualita* from the last Soft Cell album *This Night In Sodom* (1984), scintillates with an imagery peculiar to this New York drag club. 'O.K. so it's a ham/But she means every word/In a ten minute ballad of despair and blood/With one hand to the bosom/Paid for by the ballad...' And no-one but Almond would have risked a chorus stating, 'I'm so sick in my spare time humouring thugs/We could go out to dinner but we're always on drugs.' These sentiments were unlikely to endear him to the establishment, and Almond's career has been a consistent fight against censorship, many of his best singles like *Ruby Red, Mother Fist,* and *What Makes A Man A Man,* having been denied air play. But no matter the disaffection of successive record companies, Phonogram, Virgin, and EMI, Almond's inimitable voice has remained unsuppressable. Even in the periods when commercial success has proved impossible, his voice has lived as a constant reminder to the less committed that given just the right break, and he will be back on top.

Sometimes, when the mood takes me, I lie on the floor and listen to one of the takes of *When I Was A Young Man,* the anonymous poem or folk song which Almond occasionally inserts into a live set. The lyrics were thought good enough to be incorporated in *The Rattle Bag,* an anthology of poetry put together by Ted Hughes and Seamus Heaney. Almond's poetically sensitive reading of the song transforms the latter into a universal elegy for youth. His ejaculative 'I'm bound to die' travels deep into the listener's unconscious, setting off the association of white roses in a graveyard with the sort of thin denim-blue sky one imagines as the backdrop to burial. It's always cold when the earth opens to admit a body. The live points generating heat are words, song.

In character with his predominantly lyric concerns, it seems natural that Almond should turn to poetry to provide collateral extension to his own compositions. His live interpretations of Baudelaire's *Remorse Of The Dead* and Verlaine's *1,003* are executed in a manner that celebrates the perverse as symptomatic of erotic decadence, while the Latin hedonist in him gravitates towards Spanish influences, and nowhere more successfully than in his rendition of Lorca's *Two Sailors On A Beach*. The sensuousness of Lorca's imagery, and the homoerotic impulse underlying his work make it particularly accessible to Almond's range of sympathies, and one hopes that he will come to record more of Lorca in the future.

To Almond aficionados it's the compellingly funereal suite of songs *Violent Silence*, performed and recorded at the Bloomsbury Theatre in September 1984, as part of a Georges Bataille festival, which comprise the singer's most extreme statement on the nature of death, evil, and sadomasochistic relationships. The songs could have been written in rat's blood, so broodingly malign are their confessional revelations. Their contents are never sensational, they speak truthfully of a passion which is unassuagable by sex, and sees murder as the only possible catharsis to an emotively twisted rage. The songs unfold in the manner of reading a secret diary page by page. The tone is intimate, the imagery unsparing. 'I was dragging your face around the room/Somebody's boot-heel in your mouth.' The cigarette burns on the person's tongue leave no question as to the S&M ritual involved, but Almond's voice imparts a poignancy, a suffering on the part of inflictor and inflicted which lifts the material to the status of elegy. The twisted motives in the relationship described are irresolvable, but what Almond succeeds in conveying is the helplessness of both victor and victim to extricate themselves from a seething emotional arena. *Violent Silence* owes something not only to the writings of Georges Bataille, but also to those of Jean Genet – and it is the latter's concern with making a poetry out of spiritual degradation which finds a close parallel in Almond's creative psychology. Both men would find a red rose appearing from a crack in the pavement, or hear a drowned man singing in the river's undertow.

In a real sense, Marc Almond is still only beginning. His

prolific recording career is small in terms of the material he would like to offer us, if only a sympathetic record label would give him the unpressurized freedom to pursue an uncompromising commitment to song. Giving one's life to one's art is an isolating and often disparaging experience. It may offer the realisation of inner truth, but making the connection to a material world is a different thing. A media-dominated democratization of the arts has made it difficult for the individual to find favour. I believe it's only through the latter that great work is created. Marc Almond stands alone amongst the singers of his generation. He has rightful claims to genius. When he leaves the stage we're alerted to a redder sense of carnations, a memory of love, or many loves, and we're just a little wiser to the death which lives on the other side of the mirror.

STAIRWAY TO THE SKY

Diagram B

A blue sun sets over capital A:
the riverbed's a pyramid of cars,
scrapped metal, rusty exoskeletons,
they haven't driven Jayne Mansfield's away,

her sports model is tagged. The president
walked out of a blank television screen
and knew his office, what was expected
of his ghost writers. 'We are here today
as we have never been.
The best suit to match a blue shirt is green.
The tie is variable. It snows with spots.'

Someone still tries for mussels at low tide,
a tree grows like a deer's horn from the sand.
The breeder in the disused nuclear plant

will sell you one and three months old
mind-reading ocelots.

Jazz Riff

A jazz riff breaks from a low flying cloud.
The beach is zigzag zebra-striped.
Pelicans fly over the yellow rocks

encrusted by lichen patches pronounced
as coloured squares on bleached-out jeans.
The lighthouse is cockle-shell white,
someone works at its walls on scaffolding.
The seascape pushes to the eyes like glass.
A blue, vitreous, haze-fuzzed
disorientation. If there's a boat,

it's too far out; an improbable dot.
I look for balance on the shark-finned reef,
and thinking is like running on the spot.

I write a postcard. I'm in blue country,
the place you call Île Sèche. There's no-one here.
A T.V. set is on under the sea.

Fire Stairs

They fish tented by turquoise umbrellas
into the still; the pond a contact lens
buzzing with gnats as yo-yo micro-dots;

the city's back behind them, flexi-planes
in which the plutocratic snort crystals
to maintain power round the clock. The dead
buried in champagne-coloured ice
retain their splay of credit cards.
Someone somewhere's reading an autocue,

fixturing words. The sky is burnt-sienna red.

His wife sips honey. It's the elixir
used to preserve pharaohs. Outside, the car
waits to transport her to a room
with two-way mirrors. She is 43,

last year they told her she was 17.
The men keep fishing, aiming for smoke-rings
a trout's mouth lips across the baize-cloth green.

Red Voyage

The boat drifted for ever. It was new,
the white rocking horse discovered in the attic,
the packing crates which read China,
1939, 1943.
Arms or an annual consignment of tea?
the seals unbroken. But to catch the drift,
go with the voyage through so many seas
was more an act of imagination,
red birds breaking out of an emerald cove,
thunder crashing above the gulf,
lightning standing on yellow stalks. One day
at sea's not like any other,
the wind's contentious, contrary,
a letter, a love letter, falling down
from no explicable source. Anne-Marie
to Billy Boy signed in magenta ink.
Meanwhile, they open the attic window.
A vine points a green finger through.
The voyage gains, while they are thinking how
red skies must be raging now out at sea.

Stairway To The Sky

Some breeze, with green and yellow tree banners
superimposed on the transparency
that distance always seems. They went that way,
a road-map balanced on a jutting knee,

a white house with a woman at the door
waiting as though in a Hopper painting
for the world to arrive like a wave run
inland from the ocean right to her feet

as an expression of reality.
She picks a red fish from the blue prism,
a spotted shell, a waterproof letter.
Her life is different now. She goes upstairs

and packs. Her nipples are anemones.
She writes a note to herself, 'I'll be back
in time to watch the house gutted by flame.'
A red butt tossed into a dry prairie.

The car has gone. The landscape opens out.
He ducks his gelled head in under a frame;
the omlette's blue just like his polaroids.
He eats, staring at his own photograph.

He knows she's thinking of him in the sky,
looking out up above the clouds, en route
to crossing the time-barrier.
He keeps her image compact in his eye.

The car returns. They've been away so long,
the young man's hair is white, while she is blonde,
ten years younger than when they started out.
They pull up short. Cattle kneel by the pond.

Red Time

When the junk sank in quick yellow eddies
I was reading Michaux so far away
I could smell the ovened bread in a bakery
in Montmartre or Fiesole –
red money sinking with red sails
upriver from nowhere, somewhere today
in a place like that with a little shack
occupied by a customs man
smoking his life away on a wicker mat.

I slip a tie knot and read 10 letters.
I'm uninformed, disconnected from how
the universal wires communicate.
The messages transmitted by nerve cells
are aimed so multiply, so diversely.
Red time, or blue or green or gold. Take black.
The camera lens learns nothing from deep space.
The customs man keeps inhaling vision,
the little poppy seeds that fuel his mind.
The world around is oblong, square or flat.
I read its crazy mountains in his face.

Reading Frank O'Hara

Those wide, enthusiastic latitudes
in which the poem takes on anything
and everything, it's like meeting a friend
one's imagined, but never known,
somebody walking a beach in the wind
crazy with ideas, or at his desk
getting the lines in snatches, wasp-buzzes
of energy between the telephone,
social engagements, the subject of art.
And perhaps, more than anyone you found
expression for the very modern life
we lead, in which leisure's a luxury
and reading time reduced to minimal.
If poetry's a fast shot to the nerves,
a sort of bunchy purple animal
we hold a moment and let go, then yours
answers to that criterion. It's there
and purposeful, got down like a love heart
in which one reads the names and dates
on both sides of the arrow, then stand back
out of the headlights swishing at the wall.

Moving Lands

I'm taken by surprise. Last night the trees
crowded in on the sleeping town, got there
as though they'd walked out of a dream
into reality. So too, the lake
is central to our square, its flamingos
pooling a red sun. Will the mountains find
foundations nearer to the park
and office girls look out at violet peaks,
and then the whole scene change again,
autumn so red it's like a glass of wine
held to the light, and bringing with it men
who claim we must prepare to leave
the planet – and the routes are mapped
all the way to the stars? Everything's possible
once we abandon fixity,
and the rose which you snip, conceals inside
a mirror in which your identity
amazes, for you say your eyes turn green,
your skin turns to a leopard's, and your hair
is emerald. Now it is day or night,
I go out into the forest and wait
for your appearance. Will you be a cat
or woman, and that white statue
riding by on a horse is going where?
I listen to the movements of the earth,
antelopes crossing plains, a million miles from here,
pausing, then running hard across the flat.

Toner

He films the landscape from the moving car,
totemic cacti brutally in flower,
three migrants on the move, their shoulder packs
are life-support units: the billboard reads –
'A one way system to the stars',
and that could mean almost anything anywhere

out here between two cities, the flatland
littered with ruins, nomads dressed like astronauts
floating silently into the future,
and if the sun's observed, it's a saucer,

a grey disc flipping nearer year by year.
He videos incongruous artefacts
which might have been devised by Ernst. The clouds
have come together as a mountain range,
what looks to be a scaleable summit
is dense with white cumulus.

                    His driver holds
the one direction, no detours,
there's never any chance the road will change.

Approaching Frontiers

You left your red shoes with the border-guard,
or was that in a painting, I forget,
and in whose studio? Sometimes I go

wide of the understanding which I have,
and find your feet appealing when your toes
are meshed in a stocking's black point.
The country that we crossed to was a place
where big blue cats prowled tamely and we found
two people performing behind dry ice
in a tree-theatre off the road. They were
the last survivors of a race that wound
its grass-roots right across a continent
to a heart beating in a buried pot.

We never returned to the guard. The space
we took for the sky was orange,
an ad pulsing in a cloud, and we went
barefoot like children in the sand
counting our steps through crazy cactus land.

Days By The River

It was a girl sat in the highest branch,
and in another place she might have been
a figure looking out of a painting
into no time at all except her own,

the moment as it spots up like a fly
on a white cloth. Somebody's slick canoe
opened a seam in the water;
the minnows buzzed according to
an underwater radio.
I didn't have to call out for I knew
the girl from somewhere else, another time
on such a day as this, the sky so blue
all other colour was irrelevant.
We hadn't aged, the interval between

then and now was still the present.
And it was August, her black top, white jeans,
hitting my vision, no-one else around
except a squirrel heard and later seen.

Where Were You

Your face darted with acupuncture pins,
or so abstracted by thought, its contours
are altered to a chalk drawing,
the line gone missing – I can invent you

by way of so many variations,
orange jacket, black skirt, blown away hair
lifted by a left hand, a right,
to frame a sudden shift of mood –

pensive, blue, or enigmatic,
sometimes a brightly lipsticked clown.
Yesterday I was in Copenhagen,
it's still yesterday and I'm in Paris,

and you are looking for a town,
a passage by the Stock Exchange,
where a child concealed beneath a white sheet
dematerializes to reappear

as Lautréamont with thin grasshopper legs.
One day you'll find the place and telephone,
only to see the buildings disappear
like sugar cubes in rain. I'll be too late,

even if there were flights to get me there.
Today I'm meeting you at four,
the trees are parrots with their autumn leaves.
I'll walk through streets I know to a blue door

on the blank side of a house, open it,
and have to find you by your voice,
now here, now there, the effects are all taped.
I know you're upstairs, cat-crouched on the floor.

The Castle

We built it out of paper on the road,
stopping off where a place seemed to invite
distinction by a mulberry tree,

a red rose bordered vineyard where the grapes
waxed heavily in black ringlets, a mood
somewhere that fitted with our own
speculations, building with grey paper
not stones, and writing poetry
on walls we would assemble in the end
if we could find the spot.

It wasn't Kafka's castle, something else,
no crenellations, turrets, dark green moats
or rooks ragging into the wind
up high. No torture cells, interrogation rooms,
automatized bureaucracy.

We built by fragments, without a blueprint
on squares of paper. Later we'd meet up
with artists, draftsmen who would illustrate
our progress. Ladders in the sky
were there for communication.
The harvest was red-gold. The mauve grapes fat.
A woman we encountered on the road
had sleepwalked out of a painting.
We carried on. We had our work to do,
and were the last survivors of a lost nation.

Take 3

A stocking point laid on each shoulder blade.
That was at the Pink Hotel,
intimate dabbing of toes filmed in silk,
a sensory cosmography.

He remembers the pepper-red sunset;
the hectic salad's expressionist lash
of citric colours, edges to his plate
which had him reflexively a hands-up

phased-out driver at the wheel.
Mostly he felt detached as though he had
travelled through a re-entry corridor
tilting back from the moon. He'd touched the walls

while sleeping, felt the dark vibrate like bees.
Her mouth was a red locket. When she smiled
a tiny child stood in each eye.
A bra strap snaked a black vine down one arm.

The cool wine was a quick alert
to getting higher. A touch of Chanel
behind the knees was her dressed to be out
teasing the shade from non-existent trees.

Stone Ladder

A bouldered zigzag trail into the hills;
his jeep high-stepped the worst, the lizards lay
like twitching spines along each stone,
demented lightning prickles when disturbed.

At night his headlights pushed furred moons
into the dark. Sometimes one, often two
silent watchers awaited him
drinking whiskey in white cane rocking chairs,

the woman hardly dressed, the boy
with marmoset's eyes, carving a canoe
from bark, arrogating control
over the edgy scene, letting a shoe

drop in the silence like a dice
prognosticating who would speak. The let
was in her smile, the smudged lipstick,
the clicking ricochet she gave to ice

that tinkled in the glass. He'd read her mood
instinctively, the bruised pansy
his or the boy's lips had coloured,
was livid indigo along her neck.

They'd hear him unloading outside,
and sit there tense, acquisitive. Tonight
he stayed out a long time. Stones from the peak
were moving again in a lithic tide.

Unexpected Journeys

You climb a stringy beanstalk in my dream,
the red flowers inking themselves as tattoos
over your body, arms, shoulders and back
motifed with that design, a black love heart

on your right bottom cheek. Later that day,
we flew to Paris and I found myself
checking your shoulder, expecting to find
a strategically placed flower just wide

of a bra strap. I drifted off mid-flight,
and there you were again, this time walking
through streets I didn't know, a neighbourhood
disrupted by abrupt catastrophe,

and you had taken off your shoes, and dust
poured through them in a thin filter,
like someone upturning a pepper pot.
A crowd was somewhere; they were irate bees

trapped in a loaded microphone.
In Paris, we set out things in our room,
the little indispensables
that make a home, and looked out over trees,

dense green planes on the avenue,
and you were anxious I explore
your body for the love heart, cheek by cheek,
your black silk things a beanstalk on the floor.

Explorers

They went downriver and the yellow trees
were vertical lightnings. Bugs stung the eyes
like smoke. A jet's truncated fuselage
was strung across a clearing. Who were they,

and what war emptied out this world?
Two dead alligators were upside down
at a bend in the river. 'Sail away
with me,' the voice sang on the radio

just a decade ago.
The men on deck use tripods, video
whatever drifts into the lens,
violet grafitti slashed on a warehouse,

someone tripping on acid in a tree,
naked, and waving to the camera crew.
The men are shooting a film of a film,
they can't get hold of what's reality ....

They think maybe a century
has happened since they came out here.
Childhood is liveable again
each time torrential thunder rain

smashes the deck, alters memory cells
as though clouds were spiked with hallucinogens,
a purple rabbit sits on a purple mushroom,
a green vase squats on a ledge in the air.

They hold their course. There is no end to this.
The progress that they make's illusory,
and that fat caterpillar's moving back
takes on the motion of the endless sea.

The Palace

The agency takes bookings by a code.
To meet the guide you must travel blindfold
by night in a black limousine
to an unspecified place. A pink boat
is waiting to unzip the lake
the way a tight silk dress is slashed open.
And then? A car waits on the other side,
its headlights full to signify – all's clear.
The forest road is tortuous, zigzags
between impenetrable undergrowth.
Whatever crashed here on its war missions,
torn from the air in flames was left to rust.
The last pilot was eaten by a bear?

Taped music will instruct you of the route,
interspersed with passages read from Sade,
and it may seem like days since you set out,
no variation on the speed
indicating a bend, a spiral loop.
Perhaps there is no driver at the wheel,
and the car's whizzing down the motorway
on automatic pilot. It won't crash
because there's no end to the road.
And when the blindfold's lifted, will there be
a building seen at last behind high walls,
open to initiates who revert
to youth after a three week stay,
or just a ruin guarded by a bear,
or the strip lighting above a roadway
that winds around the world in going there?

Appetite

They raced each other through the early street,
the mist hanging a blue net in the trees
and it was still an unreality

this breaking out with pieces of a dream
fragmenting like a glass dropped from a height
into a blue and red prismatic star.
A car's headlights travelled at them like suns
floating through to investigate the world,

its blank façades, a scarlet traffic-light.

And where they ran they'd never been before,
the wasteland sprung thistles around their legs,
airbrushed grafitti loops strung on a wall
seemed like an autonomous dialect...

And when they turned and walked back to the town
they'd lost momentum and the dream
they'd thought to lose solidified
around them; she was still a spotted fish
and he was listening to a telephone
ring from inside a satin box
lodged on the bottom of a stream.

Thinking About Poetry

My left foot's leopard-spotted, the right black,
one shoe on, one shoe off, I'm distracted
by a stray line that hooks itself
like pasta to a cat's cradle
of stringy offshoots. My neighbour's red car
sets off for sunflower fields en route
to Budapest. I try to clear a way
for verbal walk-ins; they've come very far
to transmit impulses. A telephone
makes signals in another room;
the sky's a roof to everything which climbs
towards the vertical like poetry,
the snake inside the rope, the rope the snake.
My feet co-ordinate as the next move,
and now and then I think how others too
are filling in the time with poetry,
shifting a city or the nearest star
across the page. Worlds move in imagery,
as though they're created metaphor,
galaxies reduced to the weight of words.
I'm all that, plus a frailty, shot nerves
and upended perspective, one window
open to jump through and race for the sea.

Stars Waiting On Mountains

And sometimes, latterly, they understand
the messages transmitted on cassette
and sent them in black envelopes.
Nearer, their father writes about the farm,
the ruined seasons and how a white horse
swam right across the mountain lake
and came to his front door and stayed.
That was 100 years ago. His snaps
illustrate how he's changed, and one autoportrait
presents a double. The child that he was
peers through a mop-haired fringe
over a bony left shoulder.
One day, the child will say to him, 'follow,'
and they will mount the horse and swim all day
and night to complete the journey.
And he will know the place, sit on a gold boulder,
leave the child fish for salmon with the bears.
The distance hardly matters.

Sometimes they write their father. 'We're not far,
but since the audios arrived we seem
detached, estranged. Last night the snow was mauve,
the couple came from a near star
and helped us decipher their messages.
We may go with them when we are informed;
and your white horse would have turned purple here
beneath the flurry.
　　　　　　　Jill's gone in her car
towards our highest peak. I'm left behind,
impatient to have news, but anyhow
what we're both doing must seem very clear.'

Miranda

She sets out shoes, gets the pink on display
beside gold sandals. The boxes present
cardboard burial vaults, black tissue paper
concealing fragile heels, toe-points
that seem too narrow for a foot
to squeeze an entry. Left alone, she'll lift
a lid and peep inside, amazed
at her discovery, each one so light
it balances inside an outstretched hand.
A leopard-spotted canoe on a spike,
white leather awaiting silk-stockinged feet,
a red meaning defiant risk.

Lunchtimes, the other staff gone out,
the shop empty, she'll dare unwrap a black
suede stiletto – it is her favourite choice –
and try one, then the other, see them stand
tall in the mirror, and her legs
adopt the curve she wants. A secret act,
it transmits a thrill to the day,
sustains her through the afternoon, the smile
with which she invites customers to try
a flat or high shoe, and the sadder note
if her own favourites are picked out,
imagining the woman later on
learning to balance and with practise float.

Writing To

A blue day opens out into a red.
An afternoon spent up on the third floor
meant reading Strindberg's mania,
the lyricism all pathologized,
the stars and stripes duvet, the black curtains
unfurling like flags with a breeze
from nowhere. Just the empty sky

waiting the way a blank cinema screen
seems ordinary without images.
And after the scenario, credits,
we see a woman tying up her hair,
a man sits watching her, he's still in bed,
despite the Paris or Berlin day.
His green jacket's hung over a white chair.
Her black bra is transparent lace.
She smiles, and now the music starts to play.

It's been like that for hours. Cinematic,
post-coital. My green-eyed look
goes once around the universe
and back to you. I hear you turn a page.
You're reading by wishing you had a book.

Interview

An archivist's depository,
he's made his house into a honeycombed
data mausoleum, papers, cassettes,
the many voices magnetized on tape,
only temporalized when the loop unwinds
and syllables articulate

reversed time. It was a blonde afternoon
ten years ago, a New York apartment,
Warhol's silver-platinum wig
starkly realized against all-black clothes.
A blue slab of sky outside; in Cologne
rain drilling bullet-holes through red tulips.
In Paris, a green telephone
urgently alerted an empty flat.
He bit a nail clean through thinking of her
with someone else. Her pencilled lipstick gloss

an invitation to draw run-up blinds.
He is the janitor, keeper of other lives.
He checks the fridge. Sardines, his frozen stash.
Something of everyone somehow survives.

Green Moods

A different temper to blue, a shade
denoting a slight up on solitude,
a green movie, a green hour, a green mood,
it's a new flavour for the cocktail straw
through which we savour life. The clear postmark
tells me your letter was a year coming,
and so much happened in between, I saw

a plateau overtaken by the sea,
and when it withdrew there were triton shells,
tufted manes of emerald weed,
a *mise-en-scène*, an improvised
marine canvas by Yves Tanguy.

I juggle a blue ball and then a green.
Your eyeliner takes up with the latter;
mascara always smells of writing ink.
The bottle-green sky moves in by mid-afternoon.
Those who anticipate it go on out
walking to nowhere, or else take a train
to a city whose name I cannot spell,
except its walls are green, its occupants

square-headed. It's an individual thing,
the texture deepens after summer rain.

The Fast

We cut the moment into two hundred
conceptual flashes. He's on Channel A
mentally editing a video
in which masked biker boys breeze through L.A.

on a vengeance mission. A big green moon
squats above dusty hills. On Channel B,
he's thinking of his girlfriend, r*ue du bac*,
her scarlet nails twist the ignition key,

but she's immobile in the traffic slick;
her pink skirt is at risk. On Channel C,
she tries to imagine his whereabouts,
he's posted back upright against a tree,

shooting the backdrop for a clip. She's late
and of course the lift jams. On Channel D
he re-edits the film. The band are seen
playing headless. On the floor a mummy

screened by Anubis, has its bandaged head
wired to a Walkman. And on Channel E
his flashback is of her in green panties,
clear as the air in their transparency.

She gets out on the 5th floor. Here she tests
skin products in a lab. On Channel F
she intersects with a wrong frequency.
The man she sees is old and blind and deaf,

begging in the subway. But it is him
in 30 years. She blocks out Channel G.
He gets the interference, blows his top.
He heads the car anywhere to be free.

Pre-Equinox

The wind pricks up a cat's ear out at sea,
horses that moved on silk hooves all summer
are snorting, ready to stampede,
a knuckle makes a tom-tom on a drum.

Words which were building crazy in the head
pour from the throat as a cloudburst of bees,
distempered blotches sit on the paper
as though I'd left the page beneath a tree

raining ripe mulberries, and if I spoke,
I fear my voice might go away for good,
burst into a kitchen in Mexico,
or live with bats hanging in a hay loft.

It's now the stone longs for the precipice,
the bull carries a red sun in its brain,
it's now you want nothing against your skin,
but a crystal twist of transparency.

The universal energies prepare
to bring the world indoors. Sand grains travelled
through aeons to reach a consistency
that lays a powder trail inside the hall.

We're waiting for the snap, the blown raindrop
come shivering off the Atlantic's back.
Your tongue enters my mouth like wine.
The wasp is grounded, dragging its tail sting.

It's time to revolutionize the blood,
watch a glass levitate in the mad air,
time for the fields to walk into a barn,
a tempest to blow out of your black hair.

Tight Fit

He looks up from discourse with narrative,
the chapter separates, spirals away
on a note when the Puerto Rican's lips
snake the woman's black bra strap off-shoulder,
and it's a different place he thinks into,
the holiday brochures for Cairo, Teneriffe,
his wife's calling out from another room
about a window that's open too wide,
he hears her taking off her shoes,
exchanging a tight skirt for jeans, the zips
transmit a current through his spine, L.A.

is another alternative, Athens,
the names that give a structure to the world,
eroded nominatives expiring
in traffic haze, acrid gardenia
of dead water. The struggle with denim
is how to fit a too close skin
over the body's curves. He juts his head
to angle through the open door,
his wife is bent over, a red g-string
neatly dividing her bottom,
jeans moving up towards her thighs, balance
precarious, and now one foot
lifted, then the other, they mutually
decide on Cairo, and his hands assist
the final shaping, as she finds her shoes
and walks now with an oscillating twist.

Stretch

The spider's highwire elasticity,
tuning resonant strings, tightening a chord
strung up from its umbilical and pitched,
is one way of expansion, turning out
the inner, so it's recognizable –

the pattern's articulated that way.
Count to a thousand from the toe to knee,
my pointed tongue picks out the lozenges
in each fishnet stocking you wear,
black mesh demanding I go higher and explore
the insides of your thighs,
the soft flesh there. We used to drive across
a curved suspension bridge, one bank of town
to the other, a green river
making fast tracks beneath. We love like that,
our nerve-endings feeling for subtle links,
a way from inside to be each other
at the interior. And when you come,

this means stretching to reach the highest note,
the one that has you bunch and ripple free
in scales so individual
they need notation as a score.
I know you then as vocable, your toes
sensitised, struggling in black net,
the spider on the window tugging hard
to fix a line, leaving the tie point float.

Neo Dadaist Cocktail

The basement's ratted. Where the skinheads lit
a fire, they've blackened in a swastika,
a prescient deathshead sits on the wall,
the more dramatic for its orange eyes,
beer cans are punched into this dialect,
declared credo, Search And Destroy.
The gang hung out there, drew chains to elect
a grizzled leader, saw the metaphor
extend beyond Hitler's bunker
to their underground hideaway, a lair
from which to issue on nocturnal raids,
unzip the precinct's loaded seam.
A post-punk blitzkrieg. They adopted names,
Blank Harry, Slash and Burn, Razorblade Jim,
and territorialized the neighbourhood,
their marks were looted windows, a sharp point
tattooed over a car's metallic sheen,
grafitti sprayed up to outlaw the rich,
a wild recriminative vocabulary,
spit in the teeth vehemence. When they left,
their ghetto blaster wrecked, one signed himself
Psycho Fuhrer. They cut into the night,
a pack hunting through side streets, born to lose,
but in the process putting up a fight.

Burroughs

Bullet holes pepper the shotgun painting –
a yellow shrine with a black continent
patched up on wood.
The suit's impeccable, no lazy tie,
the knot perfect between blue collar points,
a grey felt hat tilted back off the head,
the face vulturine, eyes which have stepped in
to live with mental space and monitor

all drifting fractal implosions.
The man is easy in his Kansas yard,
his GHQ since 1982,
the New York bunker left behind, and cats
flopping around his feet, finding the sun,
picking up on psi energies.

He's waiting for extraterrestrials,
psychic invasion; we can bypass death
by shooting interplanetary serum.
Some of us are the deathless ones. He pours
a crippling slug of Jack Daniels.
The body can't function without toxins
or weird metabolic fluctuations.
He's waiting for the big event.

And has become a legend, now a myth,
a cellular mythologem.
His double's pressure-locked in the psyche,
for fear he blows a fuse, goes out on leave
and kills. He is invaded by Genet,
his presence asks for love, for completion.
The man wanders to his tomato patch;
his amanuensis snatches a break.

The light is hazy gold. He'll outlive death,
be here when there's no longer a planet.

MARCEL PROUST AND DRUGS

At the heart of Proust's work, and few writers have afforded a more suprasensible architecture to inner space, extending sense associations to a neural cosmography in which place and time are retrieved with an almost disquieting exactitude, lies an imbalance which is respiratorial, and by virtue of that flaw chemicalized, adjusted, individual by way of defect.

Asthma, orthopmoea, cardiac spasms, asphyxiation, Proust's diagnoses or maldiagnoses describe also a state which represents imaginative creativity. *My attacks give no warning. I might find myself that very day incapable of getting out of bed, or even speaking, in the throes of asphyxiations as inbearable for you as for me and with a fever amounting almost to delirium.* So Proust to Robert de Montesquiou, Thursday evening, 4 May 1905.

Proust's intake of drugs centred around uppers and downers: caffeine for use as a stimulant and veronal as a sedative. I stress this aspect of Proust's life, for his dependency on pharmaceuticals, either as a means to psychologically allaying an incipient asthma crisis, or to reactivating a chemistry dulled by sedation, is powerfully reflected in his work. Contraction and dilation. The former involved Proust in a process of endless visual retrieval, and the excavation of psychic states with their corresponding experimental values, accounts for the minutiae of psychological perception which is inseparable from his genius. Correspondingly, dilation, the euphoria that often comes after a severe nervous crisis, the out-breath acquiring expansion after constricting panic, has much to do with the escalating spiral of Proust's syntax. His breath-flow is one in which image resonates against image, and almost always visually, so that the evocation of a colour may lead from the recollection of a flower to a painting, to a sunset, to a dress, to the evaluation of a character trait in which all these qualities are combined. And it is the imagination which creates these interworlds for Proust. Illness and chemical imbalance had him restructure the world with so omnivorous an eye for detail, that the barriers between imagined and real no longer existed, but were replaced by the creation of an interworld.

It is a matter of drawing something out of the unconscious to make it enter the domain of consciousness, while trying to preserve its life, [not to] mutilate it, to keep leakage to a minimum – a reality which would apparently be destroyed by exposure to the light of mere intelligence. To succeed in this work of salvage, the whole strength of the body and the mind is not too much. Something like the same kind of effort – careful, gentle, daring – is necessary to someone who while still asleep would like to examine his sleep with his intelligence, without letting the interference wake him up.

(Letter to André Lang)

It is clear from the latter concept why Proust was to prove of interest to the young André Breton and the surrealists, for his writing leaned heavily on unconscious associations which in turn generated an imagery drawn from the deep and clear waters of the psyche. When the connection is right, which it almost invariably is, Proust's imagery takes on the shock and colour of a fish drawn from the image-pool, its colours still vibrant, scintillating, pulsing.

Proust's letters invariably contain two conditions. *I have been so ill, I am still so ill.* He was given little respite from respiratorial crises, and like all those who anticipate the spasmic trauma of hyperventilation, or in Proust's case, a breathlessness which approximated to asphyxia, he tried desperately to pre-empt the attacks by the use of drugs. And as a condition of psychological terror, he was quick to translate anxiety into physiological terms. *For I'm very much afraid that these incessant attacks have destroyed something in my organism which will never be able to recover.*

In his biography of Proust, Ronald Hayman describes the effects of the Legras powders, with which Proust incessantly fumigated. Hayman writes:

*He may have been aware the powders were addictive –
sometimes he made efforts to stop 'smoking' – but he didn't
realise that in a bedroom ventilated only by the draught from
the chimney, the carbon monoxide produced from burning the
powders and the wood could have helped to cause the malaise
he progressively suffered – headaches, nausea, exhaustion,
weakness of vision and changes in the functioning of his
central nervous system. The powders contained atropine and
hyoscyamine, which relieved the asthma by dilating and drying
the bronchial tree, but also tended to blur the vision by dilating
the pupils, and it could have contributed to the weakness,
giddiness, cardiac palpitation and the disturbance of speech
and gait he was later to suffer.*

If there is a homogeneous drug literature, and I'm thinking
of the opium dependency in the lives of Baudelaire and
Coleridge, the profligate use of hallucinogens by Rimbaud,
Artaud's involvement with a variety of drugs from opium to
heroin, Cocteau's *Opium Journal*, the heroin need inherent in
the work and lives of Anna Kavan and William Burroughs, then
Proust is part of that chemical chain, his obsession with
alleviants amounting almost to an oral fixation. Once reality
becomes an invasive threat, the compensation is artificiality, the
adjustment of inner space to a tempo which seems
proportionate to imaginative volume.

As I'm writing this I'm reminded of August Hacke's painting
The Bright House – La Maison Claire. It represents the sort of
luminous construct to which Proust turned for refuge. He might
have discovered it within himself, the white walls and red roof,
a blue fence containing the garden, the blue wash of sky above
the house, lit up, latescent, as though a galaxy had imploded
within that space. Proust would have occupied that house.
Paintings are silent. And this in part constituted his attraction to
art, and the incorporation of dynamic visuals into his prose is
still another attempt to transform the universe into a painting.
The beauty of the writing is comparable to the finest

impressionist paintings.

As the banks hereabouts were thickly wooded, the heavy shade of the trees gave the water a background which was ordinarily dark green, although sometimes when we were coming home on a calm evening after a stormy afternoon, I have seen in its depths a clear, crude blue verging on violet, suggesting a floor of Japanese cloisonné. Here and there on the surface, blushing like a strawberry, floated a water-lily flower with a scarlet centre and white edges. Farther on, the flowers were more numerous, paler, less glossy, more thickly seeded, more tightly folded, and disposed, by accident, in festoons so graceful that I fancy I saw floating upon the stream, as after the sad dismantling of some Watteau fête galante, moss-roses in loosened garlands.

The effect of this richly textured mosaic is to show us the outer surface of Proust's nervous complexity. Information stored in the memory cells, tonal propensities, meditations on nature and art, a whole storage system which had been withheld, spirals into a reflective magnitude, a release contingent on imbalance and the creative condition on which it meets the world. Proust is in part describing the unconscious – the dark green pool in which images flicker or browse murkily like fish.

And writing as he did, under extreme paucity of light, the source generated by a green-shaded lamp, Proust with his curtains drawn on the seasons, lived in the half-light, the intermediary stage between the unconscious and its realization through writing, transmission on to the white glare of the page.

And my life is so bizarre and lamentable that whenever I talk about it I give the impression of apologizing, Proust was to write to Max Daireaux. The combination of genius and its modification through the chemical permutations of drugs, created in Proust the role of a messenger between worlds. How well he would have understood Rilke's poem *Orpheus Eurydice and Hermes.*

In front, the thin man in the cobalt cloak – silent, impatient,
looking straight ahead. In quick, obsessive strides, his chewing
walk ate up the road; his hands dropped at his sides, compact
and weighted, from the sky-blue folds, and hardly conscious of
the fragile lyre crooked into his left arm – and how it grew like
roses grafted to an olive tree.

What Proust ate up, with an insatiable rapacity, was
memory. Unable to detach himself from the past, he made the
recreation of it into a timeless present. The mobility he had
achieved in relation to inner space was in contradiction to his
inert, valetudinarian body. *I go out roughly once a month for*
an hour, and afterwards, quite apart from attacks of asthma,
have to spend a week in bed.
   The situation appeared intolerable. Constant palpitations
had Proust fear a cardiac condition, but he did little or nothing
to moderate his intake of caffeine. In September 1904, he
prepared a long, detailed letter on his condition to Georges
Linossier, whose book *The Treatment Of Dyspepsia* he had
been reading. With the scrupulous attention to medical detail
which one might expect from the microphobic son of a doctor,
Proust enumerates on his bodily functions.

I eat one meal every 24 hours (and incidentally may I venture
to ask you whether from the point of view of daily ration you
consider this meal sufficient for 24 hours: two creamed eggs, a
wing of roast chicken, three croissants, a dish of fried potatoes,
grapes, coffee, a bottle of beer) and in between the only thing
I take is a quarter of a glass of Vichy water before going to bed
(nine or ten hours after my meal). If I take a whole glass I am
woken up by congestion; a fortiori if instead of Vichy it's solid
food.

At this time, September 1904, Proust was considering
undergoing psychotherapeutic treatment in a clinic, a notion he
was to return to again and again, without the motivation to put
the theory into practice. Like most creative people, he preferred
to live with the idea of his illness, and translate physical

malfunction into imaginative gain. But from the point of view of our essay, his own analysis of his symptoms is paramount to an understanding of how Proust related to his psychophysical suffering.

My urine shows a marked excess of urea, of uric acid, and a diminution of chlorides. The analysis I had done added imponderable traces of albumen and sugar, but I believe this is quite temporary. I have been urinating very little for several years. After twelve days on a milk diet, I did not produce half a litre in twenty-four hours. It is true that I took the milk in the form of boiling café au lait, which of course greatly increased my habitual perspiration, and that I could scarcely manage to exceed a litre and a half to two litres of milk per twenty-four hours.

Proust, who in his writing, lived outside time, occupying a space in imaginative permanence, nevertheless regarded his body as a source of anguished, temporal decay, a mechanism involved in an irreversible catabasis punctuated by violent attacks of asphyxia. And if his life was a preparation for imminent death, then its quality was heightened as a consequence. Few writers have evoked the joy of living, as a transcendental counterpart to death, in the manner that Proust was to do in his reflectively experienced novel. If Proust appears to live at the centre of a diamond, out of which he cannot break, then the study of his life within those refractive interfaces is the story of someone who in Rilke's phrase, suscribes to the notion: *who speaks of winning: surviving is all.* Or as Proust would have it, true literature *familiarises people with parts of the soul which are still unknown. We must never be afraid to go too far, for truth lies beyond.*

Constantly contracted in his effort to meet the world, his breathing irregular, his diaphragm tensed to anticipate the intestinal spasm, Proust approached health with suspicion. If in terms of yoga breath represents a gift independent of man, a fluency which lives him, then Proust turned respiration into a conscious, embattled process.

If the day is fine, it is in vain that my shutters exclude every breath of fresh air; my eyes may be closed, and a fierce asthma attack, caused by this good weather, this lovely golden haze I stifle in, may almost knock me unconscious, make me incapable of speaking; I can neither utter a word nor form a thought ... Tears of pain run down my cheeks.

In the attempt to ward off asthmatic convulsions, Proust smoked Espic cigarettes and burnt medicated powders by his bedside. Hypochondria, microphobia, a deeply ingrained agoraphobia – Proust would only travel by a car which collected him – all combined to establish a reverse process of living. He set himself to visually and emotionally retrieve the past, and to imagine the present as a continuity of disjunctive time. An intensified moment in which the word substituted for distress. Proust's writing aims to establish the expansion which his physical body could never meet. It is little wonder that his novel is a house of images built to encompass the universe.

Hayman tells us that to send himself to sleep Proust used a combination of Trional, Valerian and Amyl.

Trional was a hypnotic drug consisting of an ethyl sulphone. Valerian, a herbal sedative, had been popular throughout the nineteenth century. Amyl was a tertiary amyl alcohol currently in use as a sedative.

I write this on an afternoon when snow shuts in the world, reduces everything to a prismatic dazzle. That leopard-spotted thrush is suddenly too huge, too articulate. Its jewelled brown eyes emphasize the separation of consciousness between myself and it. And it expands, grows to the actual size of a leopard, is huge, predatory and menacing under a violet sun. And suddenly I'm reminded of my own need, the Lorazepam which asserts a tyranny over my metabolism. On bad days, shapes change so dramatically with such a protean, hallucinated content that I have to unlearn seeing and retreat into self-containment. I imagine a bat hung up in a black cave. A visual shut down.

In a letter that Proust wrote to his mother sometime in 1905, his condition of stress was such that he mentions the possibility of using heroin to alleviate the situation. I quote the letter in full.

Ma chère petite Maman,

Please don't fail to have someone in this evening. Although I'm a thousand times in less pain, I'm naturally spending a far worse day than yesterday, as so far it's been impossible to rest lying down, even without going to sleep, and I'm fumigating all the time. As a precautionary measure you might get some heroin on the off-chance, although I'm absolutely determined not to take any. But one can't tell what might happen with these attacks, that are so unlike what I've been used to. So it would be much better to be prepared than to have to wake a chemist up tonight.

I feel better at the moment. I hope this rain will put me in better condition. Please get the heroin in any case, just for safety's sake.

While she was alive, Proust used his mother as a confidante in matters pertaining to his asthmatic condition. He monitored his crises with a diaristic and self-diagnostic obsession. By projecting his fears on to her, he was able to find comfort in diminishing the sense of isolation which comes about through nervous terror. It's possible to reach a state whereby a white tiger sits in one's head, showing its blue eyes, threatening one with nervous paralysis should it move a step forward, or flex a muscle lazily in sleep. Proust shared each intimate detail of his drug habit with his mother.

Back home at 11 p.m. precisely. Felt rather oppressed in spite of several Espics during the day, had a fumigation. It was my first time alone, so it all took ages. Went to bed at half-past (time by the clock in your boudoir), chest tight in spite of fumigation, took two capsules of amyl. Sleep came quickly. 5.30 a.m. awakened by oppression or at least with oppression, indeed with rather severe panting. Got up and had an energetic fumigation

with Escouflaire and Legras powders, by which I was literally...
Wed, 9.30 a.m. 2 September 1896

There was a vicious trap involved here. In order to demand attention from his mother, Proust considered he had to be ill. It was a mode of behaviour which was expected of him. His mother wouldn't have recognized a healthy son, and to be the latter would have involved letting go of the past which was so vital to his work, and relinquishing hold on a world which his imagination had frozen into permanent immobility.

Proust's work is so alive with images, each of them compounded from a deep poetic sensibility, that one can imagine the frozen quarry where they lay dormant and glyptic, blocks cut by memory cells, which at an instant were to become fluid and leap into the imaginative arena. Proust stored everything. The most complex, diverse and elusive sense-associations were activated through writing to a holistic synaesthesia. Marcel would have had time stand still, only the physical effort involved in writing demanded he entered the temporal flux, that journey in which we grow physically old as a contradiction to the timelessness of inner space.

Cardiac spasms and angina pectoris, and a serious undermining of the central nervous system due to his too liberal use of opium-based anti-asthma powders, were only some of the disquieting symptoms which kept Proust confined to bed, unwilling to take any form of exercise, and living as the horrified annotator of his own dissolution. *The torment of a neurasthenic is out of all proportion to the gravity of its cause* he was to note.

As early as 1905, Proust felt that his body could not survive the intensity of his panic-convulsions. While caffeine, taken in tablet form, relaxed his breathing, it also had his arms and legs shake if he attempted physical exertion. His asthma attacks, which were accentuated by paroxysms induced by drug poisoning, could last for anything up to 24 hours. At such times he suffered from a condition called orthopmoea, by which the person can only breathe by maintaining a standing posture.

Proust's confidence that he would outlive his condition by

writing, and play tricks on anabasis by retreat into the past are amongst the great heroic gestures in literature. And underlying his creative furor was the private myth that he would be well one day, and that life would commence without reference to an injurious past. Hadn't he also a right to live? But illness was inextricably linked to his creative source, so much so that he realized the expansion of time granted to an invalid would correspondingly represent the allocation of undisturbed hours in which to write. And to enforce his hermeticism, Proust inverted night and day, his day not beginning until three or four in the afternoon, and his writing hours occupying the night, with occasional visits to restaurants or friends occupying the hours between ten and midnight. The eccentricity of his life freed him from the pressures of social obligations, and the night as it was for Novalis and Rilke, became for Proust a black diamond, a depth invested with absolute clarity and silence, a passage which had to be accompanied by a story – an accompanying inner voice which grew to be *A La Recherche*.

Proust's doctors were many, and included Dr Pierre Merklen, who in 1904 referred Proust to the clinic of Dr Paul Dubois in Berne. There was Professor Henri Vaquez who in 1902, diagnosed Proust's tachycardia as nervous and not cardiogenic in origin, there was Dr Widmer with whom Proust took a rest cure at Valmont in 1905, and amongst others Dr Maurice Bize who remained Proust's regular general practitioner, and who advocated injection of camphorated alcohol to help relieve congestion of the chest.

What a man does in his private hours, with only himself as witness to the accompanying act can be perversely self-destructive. There's a complicitous pact in this, the notion of duality. Whatever miscalculated doses of drugs Proust took in his dressing room at 102 Boulevard Haussmann, involved the element of clandestinity by which he lived. Answerable to his mother, even after her death, his manner oscillated between revenge for the repressed infantilism she had instated in him – at the time of her death she still considered him to be a four-year-old – and a constant desire to recreate her through his writing. The misuse of drugs was one way of defying her, so too was his perverse decision to furnish the male brothel he owned during the First World War years with his parents' furniture. Jean Cocteau remembers Proust in *La Difficulté D'Être*:

Do not expect me to follow Proust on his nocturnal excursions and describe them to you. But you may know that these took place in a cab belonging to Albaret, the husband of Céleste, a night cab truly worthy of Fantomas himself. From these trips, whence he returned at dawn, clutching his fur-lined coat, deathly pale, his eyes dark-circled, a bottle of Evian water protruding from his pocket, his black fringe over his forehead, and one of his button boots unbuttoned, his bowler hat in his hand, like the ghost of Sacher Masoch, Proust would bring back figures and calculations which allowed him to build a cathedral in his bedroom and to make wild roses grow there.

Throughout his life, Proust vacillated over the probability of a cure for his asthma, and the suspicion that if he lost his imbalance, his creative impulse would in some way be impaired. Illness had become the condition for creativity. The breathless, drug-riddled organism through which he lived was preferable to health. He knew that. Asthma set him apart, and his life was lived in accordance with the idiosyncratic dictates most conducive to his work.

Proust who found insupportable 'the microbial sunlight of [his] chandelier' withdrew into a permanent state of artificial or true night. And over that imposed reality rose the brilliant sun of his imagination.

In a long correspondence with his friend, Georges de Lauris, Proust touched often on the night and illness, the two constituents integrated into his working day. Quoting St John, Proust admonishes himself:

The night comes when no man can work. I am already half-way into this night, Georges, despite fleeting appearances which mean nothing. But you still have light and will have for many long years, therefore work. Then, when life brings

disappointments, there are consolations, for true life is
elsewhere, not in life itself, nor afterwards, but outside, if a
term derived from space can have a meaning in a world freed
therefrom.

More than the persistently deleterious effects of asthma, and
a respiratory system hypersensitive to colds, flu and minute
changes of bodily temperature, Proust was the victim of
narcotic poisoning. Reluctant to accept medical diagnoses, and
Proust shared affinities with Rilke in his readiness to entertain
illness as a form of mystic revelation, he set about prescribing
for himself in the attempt to conciliate an alarming nervous
condition. And there is something which will forever remain
secret about Proust's life, it is a quality which defies even the
most exhaustive biography and it has to do with chemical
adjustment. The gravitation inwards, the fascination to live
through the unconscious, and have images form hypnagogic
nebulae, as in childhood as a condition before sleep, kept
Proust isolated and apart. Drugs create unsociability, for one's
own need cannot readily be shared, and they generate secrecy
within the user.

This frantic race, sleepless inspite of illness, this 'race
towards death' had changed me so much, I no longer
recognised myself in mirrors and people in stations asked
whether there was anything I needed ... And since then I've
spent all the time trying to recover.

When we read Proust we enter into the complicity of his
life, the complex permutations of his inner states, the private
mythology which governed his illness. Towards the end of his
life, he was injecting himself often injudiciously with a mixture
of Evadine and Kola. The latter comprised a mixture of
adrenalin and hypophysical extract. He had begun to suffer
from vertigo, speech impairment, muscular paralysis in his face.
He needed to inject himself with an ampoule of adrenalin
before undertaking any physical exertion. Opium, Veronal and
Dial, Proust like all drug-users became confused as to the
quantity he had taken each day. His doses were misregulated

and his aphasia grew more pronounced at times. The need to write found a co-tangential impulse in the need to support that undertaking by drugs. The equation between the two functions is a simple one. The man writing out of his nerves, translating his inner life into poetry, feels a corresponding loss for which the drug appears to substitute. The fear of giving too much leads to an overcompensation of support. Writing is always terrifying, and Rilke was giving voice to a profound truth when he wrote: *Every angel is terrible.* Externalising the archetypal substrata of inner space demands a courage that few possess. The risk in undertaking such a pursuit is insanity. Rimbaud walked away from the conflagration he had lit in his nerves. He underwent ravings, withdrawal symptoms at Roche, and out of his hallucinated visions wrote *Une Saison En Enfer.*

Proust remained writing to the very end. Death visited him in the figure of a woman dressed in black, and once she had entered his consciousness, the process was irreversible. It was his individual death. He was frightened by the figure for it occupied too much space, it was still another intrusion on his breathing. There was all the more reason to go. Proust couldn't have lived with an intruder. He had lived with figures from his past and the inventions of fiction, and all of these were constellated in mental space. He had the advantage of distance on them. And anyhow his work had taken on the independent life he had wished for it.

What are a man's last memories? They may be totally inconsequential, trivial, delirious, or a coherent lucency that consciousness is expanding in proportion to physical extinction. Where was Proust then? I like to think of him re-entering his fiction.

And on the wall which faced the window and so was partially lighted, a cylinder of gold with no visible support was placed vertically and moved slowly along like the pillar of fire which went before the Hebrews in the desert. I went back to bed; obliged to taste without moving, in imagination only, and all at once, the pleasures of games, bathing, walks which the morning prompted. Joy made my heart beat thunderingly like a machine set going at full speed but fixed to the ground, which can spend its energy only by turning over on itself.

SATAN'S LITANIES

Versions Of Baudelaire

Satan's Litanies / Les Litanies De Satan

The loveliest of angels, what you knew
was soon betrayed; deprived of praise, you're blue.

Patron of exiles, burnt by Long Beach heat,
you grow more resilient in defeat.

Satan, have pity on my suffering.

You who know all the secrets, help us through
anxiety and drug-withdrawal too.

Satan, have pity on my suffering.

It's you who show the lost, the ill, the poor,
paradise is behind an alley door.

Satan, have pity on my suffering.

Your discharge in death transmits the black seed
we've come to call hope. Now it is our need.

Satan, have pity on my suffering.

It's you who gives the criminal the calm
to feel death as a rose brushing the palm.

Satan, have pity on my suffering.

You know where gold was buried on a night
when God grew jealous we should have your light.

Satan, have pity on my suffering.

You know by a clairvoyant eye where wealth
is hidden in the earth, and gained by stealth.

Satan, have pity on my suffering.

You keep the sleepwalker from the dead-drop
that overhangs a skyscraper's rooftop.

Satan, have pity on my suffering.

You rescue winos from the stunning pace
of traffic arrowed for a red-light race.

Satan, have pity on my suffering.

You teach us how our frailty is best
maintained by tranquillisers in the West.

Satan, have pity on our suffering.

You coax the new-age banker to a crash
and watch his bollocks scalded by the flash.

Satan, have pity on our suffering.

You cultivate in hookers the weird need
to contract disease and shoot up speed.

Satan, have pity on my suffering.

You promote creativity, the line
dazzles with nerve-endings and starts to shine.

Satan, have pity on my suffering.

You adopt those whose black rage chooses death
as an alternative to wasted breath.

Satan, have pity on my suffering.

Street Scene / A Une Passante

The street was fuming. Traffic at a halt.
I stood back to watch a tall girl in black
dominate by her walk; the crinkled slack
of a silk stocking leading from the fault

to a vertical seam going up high...
I tensed, feeling the heat; hoping she'd turn
to meet my eye and sense how nerves can burn
a drill-hole clean through the reddening sky.

A lightning-flash, then dark. Provocative,
stretched fabrics that gave me a second birth,
contested by my loss the assertive

impulse to follow, she who left me there,
knowing we'd never meet again on earth,
and how I'd strip her, comb her waist-length hair.

The Vampire's Metamorphoses /
Les Métamorphoses Du Vampire

The woman with the scarlet lipsticked mouth
crackled like a snake spitting on red coals,
popped her melon breasts from a black waspie,
and with her perfumed tongue nibbled these words
into my ear: 'My moist red lips convey
the art of extracting a cruel conscience;
couched on my breasts old men revive their youth
and imagine they can make love all day...
Those who see me naked, have seen the stars,
my dexterity in love can entwine
a man with the persistence of a vine;
my arms strangle or crack a back, but they
are so enflamed, so importunately
white-hot on these cushions, they lose all sense
of retribution in my kitten's play.'

When she had sucked the pearl beads from my cock,
and I responding to her needling kiss
tried to twist my body on hers, I saw
a leather bottle brimming with impure
toxins from my body; and in her place
occupying the bed's concave hollow,
there shook the remains of a skeleton,
its dry voice creaking like a weathercock
or sign-board that rustily swings
in the wind on a stormy winter's night.

The Balcony / Le Balcon

Mother of memories, mistress of mistresses,
you who in pleasure mean the world to me,
and give yourself in love so openly,
do you remember home, the evening's charm?
Mother of memories, mistress of mistresses.

Evenings illuminated by firelight,
we stood on the balcony in pink mist:
the things we said together will exist
long after us. Your gentle heart and breast.
Evenings illuminated by firelight.

How beautiful the sun on sultry nights;
space deepens to a dark blue and the heart
is compelled to make out of love an art.
At times I smelt the fever of your blood.
How beautiful the sun on sultry nights.

The dark grew up around us like a wall:
my eyes meeting yours found a wildfire spark,
your tongue was a sweet poison in the dark,
your stockinged feet were sculpted to my hands.
The dark grew up around us like a wall.

I know the art of evoking the past;
those quiet hours my head laid on your knees,
and it is only through such memories
I can relive what you once gave to me.
I know the art of evoking the past.

Those vows, those perfumes. Who will save us now?
Will we relive them under a black sun
in the underworld? We have lost and won
the right to be reborn in the great deeps.
Those vows, those perfumes. Who will save us now?

Street Wise / Avec Ses Vêtements

On stilettos her natural walk's a dance;
her tight sequinned dress seems to undulate
the way a snake pursues a slow advance
to the fakir's wand; but she's second rate.

Sullen as sand, the sky's indifferent.
Insensible to human suffering
she lives within the self-consumed moment,
files a red nail or checks a diamond ring.

Her eyes are hard. They have a mineral fleck,
and in her strange symbolic nature she
is both angel and sphinx, and holds in check

her provocation. Her black g-string is steel.
She is remote as a star, wanted, free
to give pleasure to those who do not feel.

Reversibility / Réversibilité

Informing angel, do you know that pain;
the shame, the remorseless anxiety,
the nameless terrors that return again,
squeezing the heart to a crushed paper ball.
Informing angel, do you know that pain?

Enlightened angel, do you know that hate;
fists knotted in the dark, the scalding tears,
the heart's primitive drum-tattoo, the late
decision for revenge; overcharged nerves.
Enlightened angel, do you know that hate?

Constructive angel, do you know disease;
terminal hours spent in a hospice,
propped up on pillows with a view of trees,
alone and exiled, dying in the light.
Constructive angel, do you know disease?

Angel of beauty, do you know decay;
facial collapse, the fear of growing old,
the torture of reading day after day
one's dissolution in another's eyes.
Angel of beauty, do you know decay?

Angel of luminous vivacity,
David dying would have found renewed health
in the light-waves of your dancer's body;
but all I ask is the gift of your prayers.
Angel of luminous vivacity.

You'd Sleep With Anything /
Tu Mettrais L'Univers Entier Dans Ta Ruelle

You skirt-hitched slut, you'd sleep with anyone
and anything. Boredom makes you perverse
and crave for kicks; you're up all night on speed.
Your fetish is to bite a heart and spit
the pink flesh out which darkens in the pit.
Your eyes light up like a jeweller's display,
or burn like fireworks at a festival,
but lack the moderation to assume
beauty must understate itself or lose.

You're nothing but a sex-machine. Your tricks
are vampirical on assorted pricks,
your shamelessness leaves you insensible
to how the mirror frames you as a tart.
But even you in your most private hours
must shrink from what's enacted on your bed,
the long consummate nights of giving head
to clients, and the one mistake
that catches you my leather queen gives birth
incongruously to a child genius

who lives to duplicate your ways on earth.

The Game / Le Jeu

They tremble on rickety chairs, old whores
sooty with mascara, trying to hook
the unsuspecting; paste jewellery too loud
to match the film star in a glossy book,

and mesmerised by the table reveal
blue lips and toothless gums, a bone structure
picked like a chicken carcass to its ribs.
Each rouged cheek's cut by a branching fissure...

In deeper red chairs, puddled by low light,
old poets group beneath a chandelier,
their lines are frozen, acid eats their skin,
their offshore mirage island's never clear,

the books they wrote are converted to disk.
My eye turns inward, I can see myself
lodged in a corner, most faculties dead,
the new unread authors lining my shelf,

envying those who are still lecherous,
arthritic joints stiffened, their graveyard flesh
marketed for a drink, hookers whose wit
I sit and nurture with obscene relish,

envious too of those who cultivate
temerity of self, and in distress
suck poison from their wounds, and still prefer
disgrace to death and hell to nothingness.

Invitation To The Voyage / L'Invitation Au Voyage

My child, my sister,
  imagine our lives together
after the voyage to blue shores.
  To love intrepidly,
  to love and die
by the sea that mirrors your eyes.
  The misty suns
  of those thunder skies
have a hold on my mind,
  the same tranquillity
  that I find
in your crystal eyes, rain-dropped for me.

Everything there is harmony and light,
richness and quiet and delight.

  Furniture that appears
  mellower with the years
would decorate our room;
  that and the rarest flowers
  whose perfume
hints at an uncertain amber;
  mirrors which seem to hold
  the ceiling's frescoed gold,
Eastern mats, a hookah
  would invite
  secret discourse at night,
the things that lovers say.

Everything there is harmony and light,
richness and quiet and delight.

Look how the freighters lean
    their shadows in serene
canals; nomadic, seabound craft.
    And it's to gratify
    your least pleasure
they've put in from all corners of the earth.
    And now the setting sun
    fires the fields, its crown
radiates over town,
    hyacinth and gold
    before it turns brown
and night falls on the world.

Everything there is harmony and light,
richness and quiet and delight.

BLUE SONATA

The Poetry Of John Ashbery

English poetry readers tend to resist John Ashbery's work, his imaginative excursions into invented worlds, his retrieval of childhood fictions, and above all the genius with which he handles the odd, the flat, the angular discourse of contemporary life with the creative sensibility.

My claim is a singular one, that John Ashbery is one of the few poets likely to prove of interest to the 21st century. Most British poetry, whether it is influenced by Heaney or Hughes appears to be circumscribed by inherited values. Its range of subject matter, the natural world, domesticity, or the more immediate political or social tensions, risks little which is not likely to be familiar territory to the reader. An Ashbery poem may take one anywhere in the course of its unpredictable trajectory and the title may offer no clue. The tie is seldom chosen to match the shirt.

And there's a dramatic thrust to Ashbery's oddity. What appears to be the endless dialogue between the poet and consciousness, conducted in a New York apartment, never falls short of the universal, no matter how conversationalised the idiosyncrasies, no matter how personal the theme. The last eight lines of the poem *Bird's–Eye View Of The Tool And Die Co* perfectly exemplifies the tone of Ashbery's method.

> The force of
> Living hopelessly backward into a past of striped
> Conversations. As long as none of them ends this side
> Of the mirrored desert in terrorist chorales.
> The finest car is as the simplest home off the coast
> Of all small cliffs too short to be haze. You turn
> To speak to someone beside the dock and the lighthouse
> Shines like garnets. It has become a stricture.

The clue here is as much in the visual concepts as it is in

the directional pointing up of language. The past comes cinematically alive due to the pictorial adjective 'striped' in relation to conversations. The stripes, oblongs, cubes, rectangles of abstract expressionism float in and out of Ashbery's poetry. And the highlighted tonality of the poem's ending – the lighthouse coming on like garnets at the instant speech is realized, has again a filmic quality. Ashbery's poems often succeed as a series of film-frames; and the modern world is like that. We look out of the window at a scenic vignette: it might be an urban block, windows lit up like square orange moons, an aircraft standing overhead, or it might be the eye takes in nothing but a curve of blue sky, or a group of horses nervously bunching in a meadow, as a car lifts up an ochre dust-cloud on the road. We're involved in the picture. An Ashbery poem demands we go along with disjunctive fictions in our questioning the nature of reality. The present is always unknowable. We jump at it like a cat a moth, but it eludes us. We're bilocated. Who we were and who were are, what we saw and what we are now seeing, doesn't necessarily have any identifiable connection. An Ashbery poem exists because consciousness is open-ended; it neither wants nor seeks a resolution to its persistent enquiries.

All that we see is penetrated by it–
The distant treetops with their steeple (so
Innocent), the stair, the windows' fixed flashing–
Pierced full of holes by the evil that is not evil,
The romance that is not mysterious, the life that is not life,
A present that is elsewhere.

English poetry leaves me in want. It's as though there exists an unconscious censor on what is permitted material for poetry. I don't find poems about clothes, rock stars, cinema, sub-culture, the gender-split and its reconciliation; I discover whole areas of life are absent, proscribed by the limitations of post-Larkin poetry. Ashbery and before him Frank O'Hara, James Schuyler and Kenneth Koch are all exponents of breaking down the taboo surrounding the unsuitability of certain areas of experience to poetry. O'Hara has a poem on a raspberry jumper, and Ashbery's acquisitive generosity extends to whatever is here and now and within the sensory recognition of the poem. His landscapes are real and imaginary. From Daffy Duck to Mad Tom, to Street Musicians and the nut-brown maid, to a menu for the day, lozenges patterned on a shirt, the interior of a painting or even 'To the aura of a plumbago-blue log cabin on /A Gadsden Purchase commemorative cover', the element of surprise in Ashbery's poetry demands that we see him as a continuous explorer. He is the man going where the imagination leads, following on the trail of experience, pushing consciousness into areas which are untested, and returning to the page with a poetry so original that it seems isolated by its innovative genius, so far in advance of its time, that it looks back for the consolation that others too might follow this way. Central to Ashbery's achievement, and outside the scope of this essay is his brilliant long antiphonal poem *Litany* from *As We Know*. A poem whose scope takes in every facet of modern experience as though it had invented the world in which we live. English poetry has nothing comparable to this achievement. Ashbery's innovations in poetry are as seminal to the future as were Satie's compositions to the germination of jazz and pop music. Who else would dare end a poem of simultaneous but independent monologues spanning seventy pages of dual columns, with the displaced question:

Repeatedly billed for my free tape.
I've written them several times but
Can't straighten it out – would you
Try?

Most young people don't read contemporary English poetry. They don't find themselves in it. The ironic or embittered tone pervading predominantly commonplace perception leads nowhere. Larkin's disciples have ended up as prosaic commentators on their own frustrations. Ashbery is the antidote to this short-circuiting, for he heightens his subject, marrying the domestic with the romantic, the secular with the visionary.

The reader is never sure where he is going or why, but only that in the end he will get there. One is all the time about to cross a bridge into the marvellous. And it's with possession of the latter that poetry begins. One steps out of the ordinary into a corner of experience never visited before. The poem *Houseboat Days* gets the measure of this imaginative voyage.

A little simple arithmetic tells you that to be with you
In this passage, this movement, is what the instance costs:
A sail out some afternoon, beyond amazement, astonished,
Apparently not tampered with. As the rain gathers and protects
Its own darkness, the place in the slipcover is noticed
For the first and last time, fading like the spine
Of an adventure novel behind glass, behind teacups.

In Ashbery's poetry private and public worlds are so inseparable that the two combine to form a particularized universe, and one which we the reader take on trust as representing the state of affairs in which poetry lives. It's a created continuity. A rainbow leaping from the page into an improbable future. And over a long career Ashbery has gone on reinventing himself with an audacity which would appear self-immolative, were it not for the regenerative impulse in him not to look back on achievements settled, but forward to methods which are still untried. From the syntactically disjunctive post-surrealism of his early work, through to the dense texture of real successes like *Fragment* in *The Double Dream Of Spring*, to the enigmatic prose experiments which comprise *Three Poems*, through to the innovative genius dismantling the whole order of poetry in *Litany*, Ashbery has remained unpredictably revolutionary. There's no knowing where a new book might lead, Ashbery's art steps into that question, surprised to find itself situated in a place unclaimed before the poem found it, and now accessible for the first time to the reader.

I saw a cottage in the sky:
I saw a balloon made of lead.

I cannot restrain my tears, and they fall
On my left hand and on my silken tie,
But I cannot and do not want to hold them back.
                    (Friends)

Sometimes I think of the man behind these poems. Reticent, shy, unfailingly modern, Ashbery is as unorthodox and importantly there as any of the great 20th century creators: Breton, Stravinsky, Picasso. We are privileged to be around at a time when he is writing.

INNER SPACE

Where I come from the sea and sky are so indivisibly blue they appear to unite without a horizon. It's as though one is confronted by an azure slab, something from which one could take out cubes or building-blocks and get through to the other side. There's bound to be more space there, and perhaps another kind of reality, an undiscovered island, its space-age men and women dressed in silver.

I've written a lot of poems about invented places, imaginary worlds, and the need to create alternative or parallel dimensions began as a defence mechanism in childhood. From the earliest age I was determined to follow no other calling but poetry. And that's a hard one to elect. My parents were poor, my school believed in practical functions aimed at helping the pupils secure conventional employment. It was the old indoctrination. Unless you joined the nine to five bureaucratic ennui, you were considered a failure, a suspect, someone who undermined a brainless authority. But through my difference I learnt the acquisition of a power on which they could not encroach. I realized that the true world is inside me. I could go anywhere, do anything, live out fictional roles, imagine myself in exotic landscapes, and all the time the others would never know. They were preoccupied with time and I with space. I was poor in their eyes, but unsurpassably rich in my own imaginative estimation. I didn't need them, their world was inflexibly solid, it was made up of buildings, cars, material acquisitions. It was heavy, rooted and based on a system that the individual was powerless to question. So I stepped back into inner space. I was a cosmonaut stimulated by the hallucinatory colours of my discoveries. I travelled light. I could walk on Mars just by thinking myself there. Magic has that particular potency.

At times it's hard to open the door into inner space and get off the street by a direct route to a place of one's imagining.

The one consolation is that no-one can get into one's head. You're you where the real light shines, and I remember that at times of deep despair. It is the ego which feeds on the illusion that we are the sum of our external possessions. People often look quietest at the moment of death because they have let everything go. They are suddenly disemburdened of the obsession to accumulate money. Of course we all need things, but we should be able to see them for what they are; perishable and impermanent like ourselves.

English poetry doesn't help very much. It's largely disconnected from the age and self-indulgently depressing. Poets like Philip Larkin who attempt to write about classes with whom they empathize, but from a privileged condition of living are suicidally flat and boring. We need something wilder, more wired to the best elements of rock music. Something like what the surrealists achieved, or the New York School of poets – Ashbery, O'Hara, Schuyler and Koch. Or for that matter the universal poetry of Pablo Neruda. Art should heighten the senses, take one somewhere one's never been before, get one out of one's situation. I like to think that good lyric poetry can still do that, and some of you reading this might be beginning to give voice to a new poetry, one which is impatient with the past and anxious to move one.

I'm writing this at a café table on a London pavement. I bring my space here and centre it. Streets are hard places, the wash of litter, the remnants of waste, it's not easy to convert these into anything that offers comfort. And there are too many eyes. Eyes that pin themselves to anyone's distress, anyone's doorway. They stick to the face, the back, the hands like flies. One could wish the street was transformed into the path to a beach: white sand constellated with pebbles, starfish, shells. I try to use that landscape when I'm going somewhere I don't like. Bringing it to mind once saved me from fainting.

I'm thinking also of the outrageous schoolboy poet Arthur Rimbaud, who ran away to Paris at the age of sixteen and was put in prison there for being unable to pay his trainfare. Rimbaud repeatedly returned to Paris and often slept rough in the street, or holed up in squalid rooms. He tramped the countryside around his native Charleville and hid for the night in bushes, ditches. He is arguably the greatest imaginative poet of the last hundred years. Rimbaud was looking in the dirt for gold. His dream was of a country, an idealistic state where the inhabitants, mostly children, would live under the sun and be free of the tireless intrusions of the material world. He talked about the coming of 'the first Christmas on earth' – the first because it was to be realized as truth, and to be celebrated as something untarnished by capitalist greed. Towards the end of his poem *A Season In Hell* he describes the visions he accepted as reality:

– *Sometimes I see in the sky endless beaches covered with white joyous nations. A huge golden vessel overhead, waves its multicoloured flags in the morning breeze. I have created all celebrations, all triumphs, all dramas. I have tried to invent new flowers, new stars, new flesh, new tongues...*

Rimbaud was so poor he couldn't even stamp his letters. For a time he lived in Soho and Camden Town, having come to London with his friend Paul Verlaine. His clothes were holed. He used to pick lice out of his hair and throw them at the rich. He would have understood today's youth. He would have welcomed the subversive aspects of rock music as a means of exposing social injustice. He had his poetry; the people who sneered at him had nothing but a sense of conformist mediocrity. Rimbaud will always remain a hero; he instated a revolution which is still going on in our inner lives.

There are some artists who never experience life. A few quiet hours in a comfortable study or studio is they think sufficient to take on the world. It is really academic lies. It lacks truth and the authenticity of experience. Rimbaud once wrote to Verlaine: 'Work is further from me than my fingernail to my eye. Shit for me. When you see me positively eat shit, only then will you find out how little it costs to feed me.'

And perhaps what is most baffling is why we suffer? London today has returned to the barbaric premise of have and have not. Who can call a nation civilized when people in the last decade of the twentieth century are sleeping in cardboard boxes? Doesn't it make a mockery of the whole system; the duplicitous, lying infrastructures who call themselves governments. Clearly the old institutions are unworkable obsoletions. The way forward is not the way back. The only hope for all of us is to go inwards and discover the intrinsic values on which to build a new society. Most people do jobs which are so negative, so alien to the self, that they never 'live'. They function. They are not allowed to be. If we have time, and that's usually because we're not wanted by the system, then we can start the work of re-evaluating what we want from life. And poetry helps with that. It elucidates chaos. When you write a diary or a poem you're speaking out your needs. And the latter can assure a value which really does make things change. Rimbaud altered the course of literature and the course of thinking. I'm confident that inner dynamism can do that again. And then the people left out in the cold will be those who have clung like encrustations to a self-indulgent capitalist ethos. Unable to go inwards they are terrified of those who do. So centre yourself deep. Be in your own world, the one they can never reach. Businessmen, politicians, industrialists, financiers – the whole field of automata – are essentially cowards. Unable to even meditate on the profounder issues of life and death, impotent to ask themselves the questions, 'Who am I?' and 'Why am I here?' they devote their lives to disparaging those who are in search of individual expression.

I spend a lot of time walking, watching, seeing things. Everyone is different; our idiosyncrasies may be inherited, assimilated or cultivated to deal with a particular situation in life. And what is called for is tolerance. At school you're told not to daydream as it's impractical. You're encouraged to be straitjacketed within certain conventions. It's assumed that there is a world out there in which everyone participates according to rules which have proved infallible. And what is that world? Restriction. Constriction. Orthodoxy. As a child one believes that life is benign. There really is somewhere to go that's not so very different from the contents of a dream. But in truth we're frog-marched into an arena of hostility. We can only backtrack to a meaningful existence through the imagination. It's there that we're free. Life loses its ugly restraints, its conditional terms that money is the credential to success.

When you're strung out, cold, wet and hungry, and there's no place to go, it's not enough to be told that we live in our heads. It's true that wherever we are we can only occupy mental space, we can't like snails push out of our shells, but human comfort is necessary to wellbeing. And some sort of privacy in which to be. And there are so many empty buildings. Shells in which no-one lives. They stand out like gravestones in every capital.

I once offered to do a number of poetry readings for Shelter on Waterloo Bridge to stimulate awareness to suffering. These couldn't take place for security reasons. I might have been attacked. I'm not sure by who. And that's the sickness in our society; one is opposed for speaking the truth. All I can do is use words which help to alter the state of things when they meet with the right sympathies. And we need so much more of the latter. Sadly, it's only when people undergo a violent shock, some serious threat to their existence, such as illness or the death of someone close that they realize there's a flaw in their life, a big gulf which can't be filled in by money or business acumen. It's the big black hole in ourselves. If we realize it's there then we can set about life as a sharing, healing process. Giving is the only action which makes sense in life, for in doing so we acknowledge our own limitations, our own vulnerability. Witholding is a form of illness. It means taking on too much weight. Thirty houses on the left shoulder, thirty on the right.

If you're standing with your back to the wall, rain knuckling your face and hands, you may wonder what use poetry is to anyone. But there is a way of building with words, of getting them into the generative current of a new future. It's obvious to everyone that we're not advancing, and that war remains an economic strategy for leaders who make of it a form of legalized murder. We're nine years from the 21st century and the same old injustices go on. If we don't change, it won't be fires under the bridges but the incineration of the planet.

In his proverbs of *Heaven And Hell*, William Blake wrote,

He whose face gives no light, shall never become a star. This is a good way to read the world. Those who carry the light can change the universe. We've got to hope they do it soon. I keep a piece of paper in my pocket. It's a message to myself, an Eastern thought from the Upanishads. *They have put a gold stopper into the neck of the bottle. Pull it, Lord! Let out reality. I am full of longing.*

WIRED TO VISION

Jeremy Reed

Mostly he's misconstrued. The imagery
is loaded, nerves wired to a lightning storm.
He's all about fast energy,
and wears an edge to the establishment,
those who rub shoulders with KY jelly,

obsequious back room boys who verbally
fix mutual favours. He's outside all that,
keeps clear of literary events,
lives for the heightened moment, admission

to the dream as it slows to show
the windy forest seen by a deer's eye,
the fly's shimmer as it attracts a trout's
swiping enquiry, the world as it's known
by opposites, by empathy.

The labels given him don't ever fit
the person or the writing. He's a myth,
a very modern one, in the making,
an outsider, not pinned against the wall

by wooden-minded hacks, but someone free
to go beyond frontiers, sit out and wait
for his imagined universe
to become in time a reality.

Camping

Black lava blocks litter the sand. She reads
a hologrammic letter. He's absorbed
in a mid-seventies Ballard,
the solitary schizoid protagonist
in pursuit of disembodied sex,
Monroe, Elizabeth Taylor.

They've parked their helicopter on the dunes;
red ibis spill on the polluted lake,
a big scarlet umbrella of dead birds
scumming the surface. Back of them and higher up
someone's built out of planetary bits
an observatory. They can see the man
telescoped into depth-space. He has lost
all notion of the earth; his body's thin
as a stood-upright laser.
He only lives on purified strawberry soda.

The two are out here camping; and indifferent
to the earth's authentic breakdown,
pursue leisure activities. They are
alone in the unfamiliar. A star
is burning greenly overhead.

They fly back to wherever is their town.

Michael Jackson

He wants to be La Toya. It's her face
he copies by the line, a geometry
that eliminates gender, points the way
to a reconstructed species. He's high
on dance, the generated pheromones

leave him ecstatic, it's a solitary
exploration of inner light, the beat
of an automated android consumed
by mirror images – he's reflected
everywhere in the mansion, and his feet

won't walk, they look for rhythm, instate speed.
Reclusive, air-sealed by security,
a legend to himself out in L.A.,
surrounded by pharaonic monuments,
an emperor's exotic menagerie,

Hollywood mannequins, he's grown into
the ultimate parody of a star,
military jackets splashed with braid, his eyes
shielded by dark glasses, a permanent
regression back to youth – how can he age

inside the dream that he's alive? He sits
beside a panther. He's always on stage.
The world outside is a receding point,
an abstract notion, and the drum machine
is on, computing faultless dance-floor hits.

Elvis Presley

He's photographed against a Cadillac,
one of the many littering his park,
white shoes conspicuous against the black

jacket, the cliff edges around the quiff
broken by gelled strands, loose diagonals.
His posture's always informally stiff,

it seems to say, 'I am the first and last
to make music into a religion.
My virtue is in owning to no past,

and yet the present leaves me obsolete.'
The antebellum façade at Graceland
has two stone lions guarding the retreat;

the rooms are kitsch, an ersatz movie set,
no sound, no light, and yet the mise en scene
describes the man: wall to wall mirrors vet

the ostentation without commentary.
A red room, blue room, chandeliers, peacocks,
each piece has no familiarity,

but suggests someone filling in a space
eclectically, obsessed by the unreal,
catching sight of himself in a surface

in which a sculpture preens. His fall was long,
cushioned by chemical supernovas.
We listen. Who is that inside the song?

Orange Pie

Later, they said the town had disappeared,
its bottle-green siesta dreams, alleys
connecting by sharp right angles,
a road leading through an arch to the sea,
the jetty busy with lobster traffic,
bollards, an incongruous obelisk,
the tourists snapping abrupt scenic shifts,
somebody on a flat roof looking out,

first one direction, then the next,
as though checking blue corners of the sky,
and gone back in to what interior,
feet feeling for the long way down?

The whole place moved away and off the map,
the way we talk of a dead friend
as still somewhere that's everywhere
and nowhere, bleached out of the air,
but existing as a thought-form
inside the light, an abstract impression.

It's in the novelty of orange pie,
savouring sharp surprises on a spoon,
that we remember white walls, a long noon
that seemed extended to a year
in a small coastal town, children and cats
tucked into doorways, and evoke the dark
that never really fell, and how statues
walked for an hour across the public park.

The System

The lozenge fizzes an expiring plume
inside the tumbler. From the 13th floor
he nurses hints of a jabbing migraine.
A helicopter brings the afternoon

indoors, an urgent day-glo messenger
aimed for a penthouse heliport, he knows
the woman pilot from the shocking-pink
logo around the new-age cryptogram

which might have been a lettrist shape poem
updated to a gay preference, a sign
to the converted. He decodes the disk
delivered yesterday – the screen graphics

informing him of geopolitics
encapsulated within DNA.
His robot secretary is on leave,
gone to a Brain Feed clinic in L.A.,

he has to readjust to the human,
the interaction of such complex moods,
the shadow bra straps beneath white chiffon.
Or is it simply drag? Another man.

Little white needles stand up in his brain.
The glare is like a snowfield. Now she's back,
the pilot insecting above his roof.
He follows the familiar sound-track,

her touch down and immediate ascent.
Most buildings are empty. A robot stands
out by the safety-rail. His silver gloves
show blood stains over artificial hands.

Leaving It All Behind

A spotted leaf tags the window,
a snick of leopard skin. Someone across
the way draws an orange curtain
to keep their concentration in, maintain
the light that feeds their creativity,

the little red fish that swims round the head
all day before vision goes dead.
This someone designs hats,
a milliner's felt, surrealist games.
She lives with 13 cats.

There are so many bizarre impulses,
nerve messages transmitted everywhere
at every moment. And my food is blue
if eaten imaginatively,
marine colours, a turquoise artichoke,

a slice of dark blue bread.
Ideas are buzzing in the air,
and when the lightning crackles energy
translates the concept. It's a man-sized bee

I pass on the street into town,
the first, or are there others? A friend's poetry
evoked that image yesterday,
others may be sitting on park benches
the way French lovers do. A new species.

The orange curtain won't be drawn all day,
although I'll invent what happens behind
that screening. A woman and 13 cats.
The biggest has one good eye, one eye blind.

Rain, Metre, Late Geraniums

In someone's novel now, a yellow cat
escapes across the page. It's autumn there,
two girl students stand looking out to sea,
grey raincoats belted at the waist,
a hand piling back russet hair,
books crammed into a canvas bag;
one reads a letter and they share the words.
He loves her, but in such difficult ways.

It's autumn here. Flash red geraniums
are brighter for the early morning rain;
the squirrel scratches on a trailing vine.
The girls are standing on a Spanish beach,
the novelist sipping an expresso
to savour smell, and sight and touch.
He'd like the one who has the greenest eyes
and reads Neruda. He imagines her
riding naked on a black horse
with flying leaves spilling into her hair.
Or rather I conceive the narrative
I'd have him write. He feels the need
to outstrip what he's done, create a life

that's sharp as halving an orange,
bright as the dancing raindrop in an eye.
I take his theme up. Clouds come tumbling back.
A giant sunflower looks up at the sky.

Evian

Four bottles standing where it's cool,
distinctly modern, less ostentatious
than Warhol's Campbells Soup, red lettering
beneath blue French Alps. Hugo Ball
might have made a sound poem of its name
at the Cabaret Voltaire, Huelsenbeck
punching out eye holes in the paper bag
over his head, discharging blanks

at individuals, while a piano stomped.
Ev
ian. As though I called out in a dream
chasing a girl the length of a white street.
It's snowing in Evian in Mont Blanc,

she left her shoes by a canopied car.
Our plastic bottles stand on the black floor
beside the fridge. I think of clarity;
pure water is unclouded thought,
the mind gone meditation-blank,
not trying to connect with anything.

By the morning four bottles will read three.
We've shared the absent one. The glacial sand
the source filtered through somehow lives in us.
We're quickly down to two then one.
Last night I re-entered my snowbound dream
and woke to find a full glass in my hand.

Coca Cola

The logo's part of a mythology;
red lip fibres imprinted on the glass,
she lets the wind find her scattered parting,
distribute unconscious changes of mood,
fly away issues by the sea.

A tangy zip that seethes along the tongue,
the palate anticipates high summer
and finds the memorable return,
last August and the one before,
June or July tasted through a striped straw.

A subtle bite imparted by the fizz,
meaning's like that in words or anything,
and later on the aftertaste transfers
to the mouth's hidden undersides, a sting.

Light Years

His mind travels on white particled dust,
cocaine as it places him somewhere else,
authenticating red quasars
outside the galaxy. He found his car
floating with space junk up above the world,
metallic deposit of dead orbits,

unmanned, defunctive probes. He was first
to be there. Later on the beach
was fidgety with hatching sea turtles
pursued by ghost crabs, foxes and racoons,
they gunned their way on fast instinctive cues
towards the wave line. There were triple moons
over Florida, blue, red, green,
that night of wild, scrambling activity,
turtles heading out into the Gulf Stream.

And he was in the city, driving round
looking for a friend's silver house,
the one papered inside with song lyrics,
wall tanks of meteoric fish,
two robots seated in the studio,

if it was ever there. Or blue, spheroid,
at the end of another road
where light was travelling away
to meet the reincarnated James Dean.

Heading To Midnight

I read the images back into day.
The green-draped bird-cage in which I have kept
the poem in its changing moods, colours,
its blue and gold feathers speckled with blood,
a snake occupying the space that words
have left, becoming something else. We slept
through a siesta. I entered your dream
as though I'd pierced an egg, gone in and out
with no perceptible fissure showing.
I found you in a crowded market place
and you weren't conscious of your orange dress
or of the man pursuing you. The street
was an impasse, boarded up black windows,
a violin-maker eating strawberries,
his face changing to a lion's. I left
before another sequence stabilized,

and carried what you'd dreamt for me over
into my poetry. That's you, that's me
I reassure myself, still looking back
at your oneiric metropolis, sure
this was an undetected invasion,
or will it be returned, your breaking through
my barriers tonight. Where will I be?
a pilgrim lighting a candle on the Ganges,
a man desperately searching through baggage
piled on a quay to find his dead father
inside a burial-ship, a crocodile
asleep on him? Now for the moment we
listen to flurried hail scrunched by a car,
a knuckle-rap of granulated ice
draws a white sheet over the road. Unseasonal
like us, surprises register,

the snake might get loose of the cage or you
appear with its gold coils wrapped round your waist,
telling me, count to ten, and the sky will turn blue.

Poets And Their Days

Words buzz directly into view or swarm
like fish into a fluent lexicon
marginally out of focus. A green scarf
picks up the light – the man's walking away
towards his private universe,
the one in which there's neither night nor day,

but light modulated by his control,
even if things jump from the shade,
a leopard, an amazing eye,
detached, advancing like a moon
from nowhere to enquire of the planet
conceived that instant in his head.
He faces it. Why should he be afraid?
A pencil gets the fragment down.

To live responsive to surprise
is everything he tells himself. The wind
picks up old paper in the street,
malevolent glints in a hub-cap shine.

He thinks the best way is to walk around
and be invaded, open to each risk
vision incurs. It all goes on inside,
a ripple chased out in flat sand,
a jungle seed growing into a tree,

and as immediately, a red Coke can
punches up bigger than his size,
its dented convex walls, a tin capsule
in which by squatting he can hide.

Notes Towards Completion

The white shirt's imperceptible wine stain,
the notion of making love after death
to a glamorous suicide –
one who was all lipstick and blown-out hair,
dead at no more than 23,
the old obsessions persist – be with me –
notepad and pen, the poetry I need
to keep myself together, all of it,
continuous, this life and that, and how
red summer clouds are now by the storm freed.

Telemedical

Direct repair. He tells me it's like that,
pharmaceuticals are too slow, defer,
but never heal. I feel the drug give space
to my constricted nerves. The shadow lifts,
but only for an interval.
I sense my thinking stretch the way a cat
refinds its elasticity
after apparent sleep. Its eyes follow,
exchanging one dimension for the next.
I need to connect with the frequencies
that reprogramme my impulses, index
my organic dissolution, the speed
at which I decompose. He has the box,
no bigger than a Walkman with a screen
that automatically X-rays each part,
reviews my body in the colour tones
of fractal paintings, tells me death is not
a point towards which we advance,
but something left behind. He leaves as soon,
his card's a digitally-coded message
I have to interpret. On his way back
he'll stop for mineral samples on our moon.

Right To The Edge Of The World

Red ink letters from the Antipodes,
Vanessa tells me how the surf assumes
a dominance, whiplash cymbals, a drum
reverberating out at sea
as though a heart beat in an emerald.

I went that way once, men were playing cards
at the edge of a maize prairie.
They looked at me, but when they tried to speak,
their forked tongues flickered, needling darts
hinting at some ophidian dialect.
Their motorbikes lay upturned in the heat,
I remember the insect whirr, my voice
sounding a long way off. Miles down the road
I got in under shade of a bean tree,
and later still, crouched in the back
of a battered, old fifties Cadillac.
The driver left me sitting by the sea,
and roared off in a dust-cloud of lit sand.

Vanessa writes me she's travelled so far
around an imaginary curve, her mind
has her walk in circles. If she's on top
of a lover then they rotate
in a concentric spin and lift
as though there is no gravity. Last week

a shark-boat disappeared in a whirlpool.
Her letters accumulate; scarlet words
on off-grey paper. I write mine
on a circular table. There are birds
blackening a sky that's white and very cool.

Exposure

His photophobia. The man's withdrawn,
convinced the light's a camera
that snaps his image, endless impressions
he'll meet with one day, the simulacra
connecting up with his future,
so many profiles, frontals, small gestures
of intimate self-expression, the ways
and moods on which he had no check

and were just him, both hands behind his head,
face tilted upwards, looking down, around,
mostly dressed in black, seen disembarking
from an engines-switched-off 747,
or self-conscious with a loaded basket
at a supermarket check out,
always appearing as someone unfound
by any place or time.
                                    He keeps inside.
His friends are xeroxed, photosensitized
each time they step into the street.
He works at design on a drawing-board,
outrage to startle the catwalks, his mind
busy with colour and line, fabric, cut,
warding off the recurrent fear
he'll encounter his life on the big screen,
ten million of him, each one very clear.

Ruins

A man stands looking down, back to his car
parked off the road. Up high, a pressured surf
stays in the pines as sibilance.
The ants are looking round the sugared tilt
of a scrunched Pepsi Cola can.
When the politicos were here, their words
were little meat cubes dancing for the pan,
the universal fry. Paparazzi
buzzed on the road. At night, a rinsing star
had someone flashed. All the windows are out,
the blackened smudge left by a fire
has run an earthquake fissure down one wall,
creepers intrude as wirings, green feelers,
and in the swimming pool a lizard suns
on cerulean tiles. A coup,
a hand pulling the plug on assassins
from the inside? We'll never know, a mad
bull-storm of psychopathic energies
eliminating, unable to stop?
The man maintains his distance, keeps his gap
as though prodded back by a charge,
a nervous fencing off from what happened.
A grass-snake uncoils by a stone,
the broken mirror in the grass
splits a cloud into eight reflections.
He stands a long time and is almost scared
the ladybird alighting on his hand
is a blown fleck of blood. There's no-one round,
the wind is up, hunting across the land.

Footnotes

Three women lying in a triangle
brushed by the yellow poppies near the shore,
an oak relegated to the background,

their long legs arched towards the sea,
and scorpions, lacquer-black, pincer-tailed, meshing
beside a stone, as Bunuel got
a scorpion-chapter for the lens
in *L'Age D'Or*. Nothing but the whoosh of surf
advancing from an emerald bay.
A visible wreck hobbling in the swell.

One wears a black rose petal as a bikini,
the second, three gold sequins placed strategically,
the third is naked. These are special days,

and there's no knowing if the world exists
around the coast, or if it's disappeared
in ways given in *Footnotes: see P.3*.

And Yellow

A dress by Matisse. It is very you,
becoming to black hair, Latin pigment,
and on the pavement in that bucket splash
are yellow tulips, almost tangerine
or gold, a lively March or April dash,
a vibrant flourish.
                    It is green and blue
that more importantly belong to me
in nuances of my inner spectrum,
a favoured, rich tonality.

Just imagine a tree of canaries
taking off into the sun; a black lake
for contrast involved in the scenery,
or a great sunflower acreage grown tall
as fir trees, heads periscoping
into the light; a child shinning a stalk
to perch in the corolla like a bird.

I ask you to invent a yellow myth
for who you are, and what happens today
in your taking the town by storm and eyes
inventing grammar for your special walk.

Looking for Faces

For you with your blonde hair, you with your black,
hoping we'll intersect again,
for years ago mean days to those we love
in one of the so many special ways
which individualize. I'm back in town
and check my reflection in shop windows
to see how much I've changed, and blue and brown
chiffon blows over as the harbour sky.
The past is like a revolving swing-door,
the faces out of sync materialize
in endless variations of themselves,
or I recall them by a record track,
the vocal transit when a saxophone
intrudes, so off-beat, tormented it might
be played by someone drowning, beyond reach.

I loiter in the old bars, new cafés,
or follow one of ten roads to the beach;
the sea's so far out it's a denim strip
behind steeple-finned, spiny reefs, black-mapped
with wrack. And I enjoy the solitude,
pausing to find an elephant's tusk shell,
a rayed artemis, and go with the mood
back to the streets around our old market's
circular cornucopiea of fruit.
I know I'll be rewarded, and prolong
my ritual, re-initiation rite
to ways and habits I adopt when here,
catching the past by its elusive tail,
shed like a lizard's so often, my grip
holds on to nothing; but it's five o'clock
and from the docks I hear a siren wail.

Days Under the Volcano

Her letter extends eight pages a day:
the climate, ashes dusting from blue sky,
the man from Milwaukee who came to stay

and wore a white suit with a white sun-hat:
an airforce pilot joined him for a week.
One threw a silver ball, one raised a bat

and there was ballistics. And latterly
a procession of black cars left the town.
The manager said, 'Keep the memory

of things like this, for they never return.'
A shot rang out clear in the afternoon.
The beach packs laval embers like an urn.

The mirror courts my preoccupation,
dressing for an imaginary lover.
Red lips, a little black dress, a station

tuned in to French radio. It's a pose,
this waiting for a woman who will give
me a man's touch as well as a red rose.

The days are wide and empty. Is it fear
has me imagine a detonation,
or that the hotel's empty. No-one's here?

Last night, I thought I saw the red cone glow.
Today a wick of smoke joins with the clouds.
The cars have come back, and they're down below.

Arriving By Wind

Most expectations find their earth that way,
delivered spontaneously in a field,
or recovered on a night road, gold box
that has the car slow to a measured stop,
the wind around relaying messages
telling me, go place a left ear
against a hollow tree, or by the steps
dropping to the subway, you'll see your name
written on a pink envelope,
but only open it after five days

for news you want, the message on the page
will be re-ordered in that time.
The wind's a cone if I embody it
subjectively, look to give expression
to how today it's much higher than me
and sounds like a squirrel flipping through leaves,
conspiratorial, out of the way.
And I remember hair poured back, your face
taking on meaning I had never known,
configurative dimensions, your lips
open as though to receive speech,
October scattered in red, strafing leaves

over both shoulders. I hold out my hands
and feel for shapes, a frightened animal
sits in my palms, prickles with dabbed cold spots
and goes as quickly where the next gust lands.

Mullein

That yellow jump into the air
with orange eyes. And it just holds its own
like fashion this year is a yellow hat

modelled by this one flower.
Sometimes I sit up all night and a train
intersects with my waiting. 3 a.m.
Its night freight comprises nuclear waste.
I follow it in sound, then imagine

a lover's face. Her eyes are violet slits.
She tells me in her dreams her ludic fantasy
was watching how her hands and feet
levitated. Looking down from the ceiling.
She had a train to catch at 3 a.m.
The end of the idea was the sea.

I try to think of mullein in the dark,
its distinctions subdued, and then the light
is at the window. Green and blue.

They're tall as me if I go back today;
but I won't find the place, their yellow hats
tilted above an ultramarine bay.

Anemones

The stem snakes up from vertical:
undulant plum-sheened crook
and coil, glossy ophidian
mimetics,
      some have a swan's neck
presenting a black-eyed
scarlet or indigo petalled
skirt, instead
of a black and yellow beaked head.

Painterly, attitudinized,
they're unconformist studio-models
that won't be postured but maintain
their own way of reaching the light
all crown like a stone pine,
straggly green underleaf.

They present metaphors;
the one chosen, the many –
a fist of water-jewels,
blue-purple, pink and red
seen as a collective blaze
uplifted from a glass,

or downturned, inquisitive,
appear to be listening
to the thought I have of them
that has the image ring.

The People

I lie under the roof; whole centuries
have disappeared since I last went outside
into yesterday's concentrated light,
and found a pot in fragments on the lawn,
cracked terracotta pieces bluely glazed,
and in the back, our spare parts car
was just a little less than usual
an ordinary car, metallic shell
lit on its convex points.
                              I took it in,
the whole surrounding land, the small details,
the words arriving in my head,
and how I seemed to stand preparatory
to some big change. The heat rolled across fields,
an ant trekked to the centre of the earth,
an aircraft buzzed without seeming to move
direction in the sky. Later I lost
myself in moving images about,
and then the dark arrived, and later sleep
after the bats, and now this altered earth
which I don't properly recognize,
but try to trust, a red monkey-faced bird
warning me off, and I'm three times my size.

In The Wind's Eye

The thin sky and a point of no return.
They'd known this mountain air before,
the aircraft ominously voluble
reverberating in the still.
She'd sewn a loose stitch in his leather jeans,
symbolically connecting two stray thoughts.
Each time she closed her eyes, a door
stood partly open, the empty white frame
balanced on a summit. A thin woman

stood waiting on the other side,
a blue jewelled clasp around her waist,
such effortless balance at such great height,
she might have been the issue of a drug,
but stayed, as though a fixed image
was there to the exclusion of all thought.
Her mouth was blue, she waited patiently,
there wasn't anywhere either could hide.

He knew her distracted, but couldn't find
a means of access. He fished the deep sky
trapped in the lake. The fish were stars,
fluent planets, and always on the move.
He liked the clarity, breathing himself
into a natural high.
                        When he returned,
he found two women sitting face to face
across the table, both identical,
and neither wanted him, nor raised an eye.

Telepathy

I keep on buzzing you, learning to speak
through thought-waves, transmitting the energy
I might have used as speech by channeling
impulses; you are five hours back
by New York time, asleep when I'm awake
and missing you, or it's me who's reversed,
dreaming in my interior dark,
while you are occupied by the evening,
lights peaking on East 42nd Street
send my hurried white blips out to track
your receptivity. If thoughts have shapes,
I imagine them as binary stars,
a red dwarf connected to a blue disc.
Your cells are constellations, a cluster
lights up when I communicate
a charge that's luminous, and I receive
intuitive units, a displacement
as though signalled by tape delay, before
I pick up on the message. We're around
each other with the crackle of fireflies,
linking each other across the universe,
a flicker chasing off, while tumbling clouds
build to a monument outside
and print long shadows on the sunlit floor.

The Star-Shaped Federation

We stood and listened to the sun. Our square
was draped and painted for a carnival,
and seven girls, each offering a star
cut out of cardboard, extended their hands
by way of ritual to the sky.

That was the day we went down to the sands
and discovered the couple come ashore
from Easter Island. They lived in a tent,
and he had eyes in which his thoughts would show
as images: a black-out, a girl's sex,
two lemons sitting in a bowl
beside an orange, 20 years ago
in a farm kitchen, and a giant crab
seen somewhere as an exhibit,
men baling out of its blue carapace
to mount a ladder to the sky...
She stood there naked, except for a scarf
tied at the hips and floating to her thighs.
They'd heaped prawns into his soldier's helmet,
she never once looked straight into his eyes.

Behind us, the procession showed,
the people chanting as they crossed the beach,
dispensing flowers, talking of the dead,
and some in cars and some on foot,
and the whole celebration slowed
around our tiny group, and all stared at
the couple, he a hand before his face,
screening the visual relay, she stooping
to lift a figurehead out of a net.

Night Light

The red sweetpea opens a double heart,
two lids of a scallop shell. After dark
I live with the idea of the flower;
the rainstorm's more immediate,
so too the whiskey as it burns
a cow's eye on the tongue, and reappears
as lift-off in mid brain.
                              I know my sleep
occurs in shattered parts, desperate run-ins
with confrontational characters,
a lizard digging out a lake,
a ring of car-lights assisting the work.
I've rushed all the way down to meet the deep,
enquired of the universe at its roots.
I wake up with my throat punctured by pins.

My night light is your apartment window
set in another city, shining out
across the river – and I hold the blaze
between my eyes, imagine it
right where it hits, a cargo boat in tow.

Gothic

Spatulate maple leaves denting the moat,
the fish are indoors, humans in a tank,
the boy in a pink glitter thong and mask,
the girl in a see-through body,
undulating with piscine fluency
for his observing eye, the one who sits
fast-forwarding video stills
to fix an obsession at night, and now
comments, while someone paints his toenails red,
on a sealed room in the East wing,
a mirrored cell, an exact pyramid
built for his cryogenic burial,

the ice-tray inhabited by a shark
preserved for his amusement. A white rat
shuttles the carpet to be holed by fangs.
He watches the killing indifferently
and settles back as the cobra adjusts
to marking up its victim's weight. The two
inside the shallow tank keep surfacing,
awaiting his command for sexual play.
He goes over to a console
and operates a light show. He wants blue
in which to receive oxygen, a key
creates a room-sized Adriatic day,
and watches as the couple step on out,
access hot air blowers, run into towels,
and seem exempt from his despotic need.

PIANO IN THE LAKE

Short Filmscripts

[The grounds to a château. The gates are mounted with masks, the handle is a papiermaché hand, the fingernails painted scarlet. Tenebrous yews, junipers and oaks screen out the house. Two naked figures can be seen moving in and out of the trees.

Headlights come feeling the distance up the drive, as a black limousine with smoked windows makes its way towards the house. Music wanders in and out, suggesting induction to a sexual ritual, forgotten autumns hidden in the basements, bizarre enemas given beneath gold taps moulded to resemble penises.

A man dressed in a white suit gets out of the car, goes inside, and enters an underground swimming pool. He is joined by the two youths come in from the grounds, one of whom carries a strawberry in his outstretched hand, places it between his lips, and transfers it to the man's mouth.]

The Man: I've got a gift for you tonight. We're eating roast penis. A macrophalic one. It's being done as a speciality, an aphrodisiac that we shall divide into three.

Blue: Your decadence knows no limits. We've never experienced reality.

Black: What happens if we have to go out into the world?

The Man: The only reality is imagination. You can travel anywhere you want with it. You can ride bareback on an elephant through Paris, dream yourself into temple ruins on seafloors, travel between city blocks on an eagle's back. Sing for me Blue. Sing my song.

I travelled one night

on a lion's mane
through the boulevards
in the pouring rain

I met a young man
in a jeweller's doorway
dreaming of diamonds
and he came to stay

He stayed for a week
in a black feathered bed
and while he was dreaming
I mistook him for dead

I buried him down
by the old yew tree
now he sits up all night
in my memory

The Man: Don't think that didn't happen. If you went out and dug beneath the yews, you'd find him. He'll tell you his name is Fabian.

Blue: You're too strange. We entertain you, but we never know where you go, and what you do in life.

Black: I bet you're driven round and round all day. You just look at the people out of the car window, and imagine you're one of them.

The Man: I want to see you nibble the delicacy at dinner tonight. This penis is reputed to be large as a marrow, and I've asked for it to be stuffed with dissolvable pearls.

The Man: Play for me on the piano Black. I want you to find a music which anticipates my thoughts. A melody that's the equivalent of a brain camera. Follow me up flights of stairs, through deserted rooms watched over by mannequins, have me find in the attic a doll waiting to grant me extreme sexual pleasure.

That's evocative, atmospheric. It reminds me of drawing back a curtain to rain falling through the red autumn trees. Now we'll eat.

[He leads the two youths through a labyrinthine corridor to the dining room. An oriental serves at table. The marrow sized penis baked in gold foil, forms a central exhibit.]

Blue: I heard a story once, that those who eat penis turn into donkeys.

Black: Only the head and the dick, Blue. Other books say that the transformation is into a rhinocerus.

The Man: And sometimes into that most mythic of all creatures – the unicorn. I've always supposed the latter exists by way of sexual conjuration. At the moment of orgasm, we all strain to have an erection like the unicorn's horn.

Blue: Who is going to taste it first?

The Man: We will savour it together. We shall all three of us raise a portion on the fork to the lips, and roll the flesh gently on the tongue. Then we shall describe it.

Black: It tastes a little like mussels, only the texture is less rubbery. Distinguishable from the sauce is a marine taste. I'm only nibbling.

Blue: Could be prawn. Or even veal. I quite like it as a delicacy.

The Man: Not bad associations. To me it's without doubt how I imagine dragon to taste. In marine associations it's not dissimilar to squid.

Blue: I shall be frightened to look into the mirror, in case I assume a donkey's head.

Black: And I shall expect to see a rhinocerus face confronting me as a reflection.

The Man: And I shall anticipate my penis growing overnight into the circumferential width of a trunk. I shall wrap its folds round a tree like ivy.

We'll have music to accompany the dessert. For the latter we have a violet jelly crowned with the blue eye of a white tiger. An exceeding rarity, it will grant you vision, inner and outer.

[Blue goes over to the piano.]

The Man: Play the piece you prepared last week. The one in which a bird hides in a turban, and when the cloth is unwound it appears and changes to a youth as it sings.

[Music to accompany the metamorphosis]

Blue: I can feel hooves. My feet are turning into a donkey's.

Black: I too can sense the change in my body. There are horns budding, poking through my cranium.

The Man: It's really happening. My penis is unravelling down my right thigh. It's twisting its way down my leg like a vine. We're becoming the realities we've imagined.

*[Blue stays at the piano and plays the prelude to **Orgiastic Rites**.]*

Cloud Sculptures

[*A young man lounges, hands thrust deep into the pockets of his skin-tight jeans, against an alley wall in Montmartre. He has modelled his hair on James Dean, a cigarette droops lazily from his nether lip, his dark glasses hang from a denim pocket. It's late afternoon. A dark blue sky is underlit by red clouds. Someone playing one of Satie's **Gnossiennes**, can be heard through an open shutter. The young man looks to either side of him. He hears the figure arriving before he sees him. A small man, with a grizzled convict's cut, eyes downcast, and portraying the depth one finds on looking into the interior of a pot, his shoulders bunched into a leather jacket, his jeans torn on the left side, approaches stealthily. He is holding a bunch of red carnations.*]

Genet: These are for you, I stole them from a cemetery. Old habits don't die.

Hoodlum: But Jean. It's me who should steal flowers for you. Come inside, Lucien wants to play for you.

Genet: I hope he's in drag. We should all outrage society by cross dressing. The bourgeois thinks skirts are just for women. In prison, all the men are transformed into girls.

Hoodlum: Lucien's got his black Chanel number on for you.

Genet: The one that sparkles like black fish flickering in an aquarium. You see, the poet in me still exists, despite my antipathy to the literate. Poetry is the diamond one picks out of a dead cat's eye. I once told a magistrate that.

[*The young man leads Genet up an unlit staircase to a second floor apartment. The place is poor, but the interior is exotic. Peacock feathers are arranged in a vase, books are littered on shelves, various heads, statuettes, are decorated with scarves, pieces of costume jewellery.]*

Hoodlum: It's all stolen. I know you'll approve. Lucien, show Jean your black number.

[A young man seated at the piano with his back to the door, turns round. He is wearing a black off the shoulder dress and is made up with eye-shadow and lipstick.]

Lucien: Jean, I've composed in honour of you. Let me play you my elegy. *Notre Dame Des Fleurs.*

*[Music: **Our Lady of the Flowers**]*

Genet: You evoke a world I've lost, but never renounced. When I wrote about prison I transformed it into a baroque castle. A penis turned into a rose, the cold stone walls blazed with the luminous encrustations of sapphire, ruby, emerald. You've got all that in your music. Let me give you a gift.
[Genet pulls from his top denim pocket a black silk stocking.]

Genet: I want you to wear this on the hand with which you caress yourself. Those who mix with Genet must live by strange habits.

Hoodlum: Lucien has done other pieces for you. Last night we were at a drag party. There was a boy dressed in transparent pink chiffon. He had a copy of your *Journal Du Voleur* strapped to his thigh.

Genet: The young put my books to better use than the old.

Lucien: It's better to live on the edge. My music comes from there. That point on the horizon from which a dust-storm blows.

Genet: And I've seen those storms in the desert. The ferocity of the horizon leaping at one like a red tiger excited me to delirium. I had to masturbate.

Hoodlum: You'll live forever you know. I mean the word *Genet* will always be on someone's lips.

Lucien: Can I play for you again? Your lyricism has inspired me to hit the light. There's somewhere in composition a central nerve that tingles on touch. Once one has found it, the notes resonate. I've called this *Journal Du Voleur.*

[He plays Thief's Journal, evoking Genet's journey through the criminal underworld, and his celebration of beauty.]

Genet: You return me to my origins. All those years I was on the run, tramping across Europe, allowing people to pay to photograph me in rags with lice proliferating on my body, noodles of lice. And in the middle of my scar-infested body, there was something so brilliant, untouchable and lucid that it hurt people to even look at this point. The inner eye is like a concealed cyclops. It generates the most terrifying energy.

Lucien: And you'd probably say it's the same power that protects the thief.

Hoodlum: When I steal I experience the rush of an orgasm.

Genet: It was like that for me, also. I used to enter apartments with a friend. We'd be so excited that we'd have sex immediately on the bed. Often we left without having touched anything. It was simply the thrill of penetrating a silence which belongs to someone else. Sometimes I would leave with a red rose taken from a vase.

Lucien: Your mention of a rose brings me back to the pieces I have written for you. When I first read *Miracle Of The Rose* I was still at school. All these years later I've felt my way into it musically.

Genet: You touch my deepest chord. When I was inside, I was taught that a criminal was someone who had in some way defaced the world. But the universe I carried within me, obeyed no other dictates but magic. The warders couldn't see that I inhabited a mental palace. I wrote *Notre Dame Des Fleurs* on prison toilet paper during those long nights in which those around me dreamt of freedom. It was my trajectory to the stars. I made love to whomever I wished by a continuous projection of fantasies. Masturbation makes men into gods.

Lucien: Let me improvise. I'll call it *Orgasm Taking Flight.* When we come, our sensation carries us so far that we appear to levitate. Listen, I'll get the sensation perfect.

[Orgasm Taking Flight]

Genet: I go with that. As long as there's art there is subversion. We make of it a current that electrocutes the status quo.

Hoodlum: Art is like pissing against a wall, Lucien says, only that the jet is aquamarine, violet, emerald, colours that create a hallucinated emission.

Genet: I've got to be off. I'm going to Tangier tomorrow, my flight is an early one.

Lucien: But Jean, you're always in flight – from yourself. Stay a while. We'll go to a bar later.

Genet: No. Give me that packet of Gitanes, I need it. I like to go places where I can feel the physical contact of the earth. I've come to replace words by counting grains of sand. Little glittering particles. Twenty or thirty handfuls and one has a novel.

[Lucien stands up.]

Lucien: Unzip my dress, and I'll play for you naked. I've saved it until last, the theme inspired by your novel *Funeral Rites*.

[Music: Funeral Rites]

Trakl's Exit

[*A gold September light hits through the trees, so solid in its falling it resembles retrievable bars to be lifted up and taken home. The air is still and taut as silk.*

A young man sits with his back to a tree. His head is shaved, his black eyes bulge from an emaciated face. He tilts his head towards the sun. Not far away from him, his sister Grete lies face down in the grass. A french window is open on the garden. Her piano positioned behind. She wears nothing but a black bikini bottom.]

Grete: What if you made me pregnant? A brother's child might not even be human. I might give birth to a horned deer or a blue frog with diamonds and rubies on its back. The child would be a monster, a figure with both our heads attached to its neck.

Trakl: I used to think the same when I made love to you. I've never spared you anything, and I won't. When I went out in search of poems I used to masturbate into the barrel of a gun. I'd imagine you conceiving a creature which would startle the forest. It would have an owl's face, a wolf's body, a rattlesnake's tail, and a huge elongated penis. People would bolt their doors against our child at night.

Grete: Do you remember how, when we were children in Salzburg, I used to play the piano as you described your visions to me. Let's do that again.

[*She runs inside from the garden, still topless, and sits at the piano.*]

Grete: You see Georg, my little devil, I'll give your monster a musical coat. And perhaps while I'm playing, he will run to join us.

Trakl: Call your piece, *Daydreaming Man Gives Birth.* [*Trakl takes a sniff of ether from the hip flask he keeps at his side. He gets up and walks towards the house. He adopts a seat beside his sister at the piano, and listens, entranced.*]

Grete: I'm thinking of the poem you wrote about us called *Passion.* Correct me, if I've got the opening wrong.

Two wolves in the dark forest
We exchanged blood in a stony embrace
And the stars of our race rained down on us.

Trakl: You remember it better than I do. And you should play it with your two fists. With the emphasis on a love that few ever know. When I'm dead I want you to play this for me. And I don't care if your husband slams the door, places his hands over his ears, implores you to stop. Make it something that he can never share. A sign between us. Something I will hear even when I'm dead.

[*Grete plays* **Passion Of Two Wolves.**]

Trakl: Now I know I shall never lose you. Even if I go mad that music will find me.

Grete: It's more likely I who shall go mad. Didn't our parents want to put me away? Do you remember the day I lay on the bed with my legs open wide, tickling myself with the white arum lily you had given me? And mother walked in. And father didn't believe her. He said that she was lying, that she was hysterical. I heard him slap her face. The sound echoed, it was so sharp and sudden. It was like cutting oneself on glass or biting into a pepper. We're a family of drug addicts.

Trakl: And what about our Alsatian governess, Maria Boring? She taught me Rimbaud, and took you to the theatre. But she was a wedge between us. She was afraid of me. I used to read what she thought of me in her diary.

Grete: And mother took so many drugs. We were a house of wolves. Mother would come back from her analyst and refuse to speak to anyone for days. She dyed her wedding dress black and lay on her bed in it. We were wolves, Georg.

Trakl: Do you remember how I would see a face staring out of the attic mirror? I would look to find myself and someone else would be in my place. An old man whose face was turned up on one side. I used to try and outstare him. There were fish floating in his eyes. A red one in the right pupil, a green one in the left.

Grete: We used to talk about a fish swimming in the mirror.

Trakl: Look, a red admiral has flown in to be with us. It opens its red and black kimono and sits in my hand. It smells of vanilla. Its life is like the blinking of an eye. It's there, but we rarely notice it.

Grete: And mother used to paint the eggs. Blue, red, yellow, violet. And father was too perplexed to comment. I did this the other day for my husband. He shouted that it was my mad brother who had put me up to this. My mad brother.

Trakl: Play for the eggs. Music for painted eggs.

Grete: You must go soon, for he will be back. I have to change. And look at the blue love bite you have left on my neck.

Trakl: I wish you'd come away with me. We could live in the forest, and stain our mouths with berries. Get drunk. Live backwards by recreating our childhood.

Grete: You must go. If he catches us together, I may have to murder him. But before you go, read me *Passion*.

Trakl: And if I die, play for me. I will never lose you like that.

By the same author:

POETRY:

Bleecker Street	*(Carcanet Press, 1980)*
By The Fisheries	*(Jonathan Cape, 1984)*
Nero	*(Jonathan Cape, 1985)*
Selected Poems	*(Penguin, 1987)*
Engaging Form	*(Jonathan Cape, 1988)*
Nineties	*(Jonathan Cape, 1990)*
Dicing For Pearls	*(Enitharmon Press, 1990)*
Red Haired Android	*(Harper Collins, 1992)*
Volcano Smoke At Diamond Beach	*(Cloud, 1992)*
Black Sugar	*(Peter Owen, 1992)*

FICTION:

Lipstick Boys	*(Enitharmon Press, 1984)*
Blue Rock	*(Jonathan Cape, 1987)*
Red Eclipse	*(Jonathan Cape, 1989)*
Inhabiting Shadows	*(Peter Owen, 1990)*
Isidore	*(Peter Owen, 1992)*
When The Whip Comes Down	*(Peter Owen, 1992)*
Diamond Nebula	*(Peter Owen, 1994)*

NON-FICTION:

Madness The Price Of Poetry	*(Peter Owen, 1989)*
Delirium	*(Peter Owen, 1991)*
Lipstick, Sex And Poetry	*(Peter Owen, 1991)*
Waiting For The Man	*(Picador, 1994)*

TRANSLATIONS:

The Coastguard's House *by* Eugenio Montale	*(Bloodaxe, 1990)*
Tempest Of Stars *by* Jean Cocteau	*(Enitharmon Books, 1992)*
Prairies Of Fever *by* Ibrahim Nasrallah	*(Interlink, 1993)*